RAISING RYANN

Book one in the
Bad Boy Reformed Series

Alyssa Rae Taylor

Reese

Six Years Earlier

"So let me get this straight," Gia's mother says in her thick East Coast accent. "Your neighbors used to be his foster parents, but they're not anymore?" We are sitting in front of my house discussing Ronald—my mother's creepy new boyfriend—when Gia spots the guy across the street.

I inhale a deep breath then slowly release it. "Yes. I don't know many of the details. My mom just said that it's complicated." I fidget a little in the back then glance out the window, trying to be discreet. "In fact, I haven't seen him in almost three years. The last time was shortly after my father's arrest. I'm actually surprised to see him at all."

She arches her thick artificial brow. "Do they take kids often?"

I think of the kids I've seen over the years. "There are three total that I can remember, but the other two were younger—a little boy and a little girl—all of them at separate times. They've been doing it for as long as I've lived here."

"Oh my God. Look!" Gia points. "He's taking off his shirt." I cover my face, praying the lawn mower starts before he hears us.

"He's tall." Mrs. Lopez's gaze continues its focus. "He looks like he could be an adult." She tilts her head, examining him. "Definitely older than you two." She's right. He is older, but I'm not going to tell her that. I'm pretty sure I've told her enough, probably even too much.

"Maybe they're just really close, and he's visiting," Gia says.

"They might be, but Jim and Pam left yesterday on business. They're supposedly out of town right now."

"He could be house sitting."

"He could be," Gia's mother answers.

Realizing what we must look like, I sink lower in my seat. "Could you guys please be a little less obvious? We've been staring at him for like ten minutes. If he catches us, I'll be mortified."

"No worries. These windows are tinted pretty well," Gia responds.

I roll my eyes. "I should probably get going." Reaching over, I grab my stuff and open the car door.

"Wow Reese, he's hot." She glances back. "I mean *really* hot. No wonder you're crazy about him."

Shutting the door softly, afraid he can hear, I say, "Will you shut up!" "I'm not crazy about …"

"He's too old for her," Mrs. Lopez interrupts, looking back at me. "He's too old for you."

"He's a man, Mom. Not some immature little boy who doesn't know how to take care of a woman." She shrugs her shoulders.

Her mom purses her lips. "Where are you getting all this," waving her hand in the air, "he's a man crap?"

"Direct TV, why?"

"Consider it cancelled." She turns to me and changes the subject. "Are you sure you're going to be okay?" Wrinkling her nose at my mom's boyfriend's truck. Mom's been working the late shift at the hospital. Her latest boyfriend happens to make my skin crawl. Unfortunately she's addicted to assholes, so it's just something I've always had to deal with.

"I'm sure."

We wave goodbye, and I walk to the door, digging deep in my purse for my key. When I step inside I find a blaring television and a passed out Ronald, complete with his hand down his pants. *Gross.* Our coffee table is covered in beer cans, and the house is a complete and total mess. *Ugh.* I make sure to grab all my things and walk straight down the hall to my bedroom.

The clock reads 8:23, and I really have to pee. I've occupied my time with a book and haven't stepped out of my room in four hours. There's no way I'd watch TV with him here, so I'm happy it's kept me entertained. I grab a pair of pajamas and slowly open my door, bolting to the bathroom before he can see me. I feel a million times better as I hop in the shower. A light knock sounds at the door just as soon as I turn on the water.

"That you, Reese?" His voice is friendly, but it still makes me cringe. The image of him earlier disgusts me. It'll probably forever be burned in my mind.

"Uh, yeah," I shout over the water, my eyes pinned to the door. "Do you need something?"

He doesn't answer.

I pause a few seconds then ask again. "Did you need something, Ronald?" There's still no response, so I close the curtain, happy I'm not forced to talk to him. *Weirdo.*

I take a much longer shower than my normal routine. If I waited long enough, he might be gone before I'm done. Who knows? Maybe it's the reason he knocked in the first place— probably just to tell me goodbye. After throwing on my clothes, I carefully comb through the tangles in my hair. My heart jolts when I open the door, and he's standing three feet across from me. "Shit!" I yell, placing my palm over my chest in an attempt to calm my breathing.

"Did I scare you?" There's an eerie look on his face as he leans against the wall watching me.

"Why are you here?" I take a step back. The look in his eyes makes me squirm.

He pushes off the wall coming toward me. "Fourteen years old, huh?" Ignoring my question, he leans over and lifts my chin with his finger and thumb. "That right?" His face is close, his breath reminds me of sour milk, and his slicked back hair looks shiny with oil or sweat.

My pulse picks up, fear settling in. "Yes," I say softly. I don't know what his plans are, but my gut tells me that I'm a part of them.

"Yeah," he smirks, eyes dropping to the swell of my breasts. "You a woman yet?"

I blink a couple times confused. "I don't know what you mean?"

Chuckling, he asks, "You get your period?"

My gaze flicks in every direction. *Did he really just ask me that?* I cross my arms trying to cover myself. "That's really none of your business Ronald."

He takes a step back. "Why not?" His gaze moves up and down my body, not caring at all if I notice.

"Eww. Aren't you like thirty-five or something?" I don't wait for him to answer, and instead, push my way through, silently praying I can get to a weapon before he follows. I tell him over my shoulder, "I'm going to bed. You should probably go." My voice comes out breathy, scared. The instant I spot the bat, I'm face down on my bedroom floor, and his heavy body is pressed against my back. As I struggle to get up, he uses his weight, sitting on my legs, pinning my arms beneath him. He's so much bigger that my kicking and bucking aren't doing anything. "Help!" My voice cracks when I give a sorry cry.

He chuckles as though he finds my effort amusing. There's a clanking sound before he grabs each one of my wrists, holding both in one hand when he wraps a cord or belt securely around them.

"Somebody help me. Please!" I try to look behind me, but he shoves my face roughly into the floor. The taste of copper fills my mouth as my teeth chomp down on my tongue.

"I don't mind you fighting, Reese." His rotting breath spreads down my neck, making me gag. "In fact I like it." He pulls back on the restraint, pushing his arousal into my backside. The right side of my face feels raw as it repeatedly rubs against the carpet; his wet tongue licks the line of my jaw and slowly moves over my cheek. "Soon I'll be inside this tight little ass."

"Please don't do this!" I beg. "My father's an ex-cop. You'll never get away with it!"

"I'm not afraid of your daddy." He laughs. "Your momma told me he ain't around no more."

Sobbing, I yell, "But he will be!" I search for anything, anything to change his mind. "I won't tell anyone if you let me go. I promise! Just let me go!" More cries come out. "I'm begging you! Don't do this!"

His face is within an inch from mine in an instant. "Oh, I know you won't tell anyone," he whispers. There's a struggle behind me, and the faint noise of a zipper. "'Cause you're gonna like it, and then you're gonna be begging for more." A blood-curdling scream fills the room that could only be mine. "You better stop screaming, or I'll put it in your mouth!" He grinds into me again, and I notice his penis is out of his pants. Pressing his lips to my ear, he asks, "You want it in your mouth, sweetheart?"

"God no," I whimper. "Please stop!"

His fingers glide up my thighs before he effortlessly tugs down my shorts. I'm helpless, sobbing, and twisting beneath him. "No!" I scream, my heart ready to explode. My eyes squeeze shut as his fingers connect with my panties. This is it. I'm going to lose my virginity to this monster. There's an earthshaking crash, and he's off me in an instant. I hear a struggle and open my eyes, finding shards of glass all around me. I flip over, shuffling back. My gaze follows the sounds of the blows. That's when I see him, my savior, or maybe he's an angel of death. He has Ronald trapped face down on the floor, with the barrel of a gun pressed roughly against his skull.

"You're going to die, you sick fuck."

Chapter One

Luke

Present Day

The bloodthirsty crowd sparks a familiar rush of adrenaline as Samantha struts back and forth across the octagon, arousing the spectators. My eyes circle the room finding Pam and Jim in their regular spot, and I'm thankful my biggest fans are here to support me. I flash Pam a wink letting her know that I see her. She grins, wiggling her eyebrows, playfully nudging Jim beside her. I rotate my neck from side to side as they announce the other contender, when Samantha pins me with her stare, mouthing the words *I love you*, before she prances out of the cage.

We stare each other down making our way to the center of the octagon. Standing nose to nose, both of us ready for them to give us the signal. I've held the last six titles in the Light Heavyweight Division. Seven is my lucky number, and I intend on winning another.

The ref spits out the rules, and round one begins. We both dance around the cage, focusing on one another's weaknesses. He's good on the ground; he'll try to take me to the mat. I'm a striker. I plan to stay standing the rest of the fight. We read each other's expressions, holding our fists in front of our faces, wondering what the other's next move will be.

I decide to take a swing, and he shuffles back. I swing again, this time backing him into the net. Both of us are throwing punches, but none are making any contact, at least not enough to count. I can tell he's getting tired, so I back off, letting him rest. If I take him down right now, the fans won't be happy. They came to see a fight, and I plan to give them one.

We breeze our way through the first round, and he starts getting cocky, doing this winking shit. It irritates the hell out of me, so I step up my game, charging after him. He positions himself in a crouch, telling me he's ready to grapple and reaches out his arms to wrap them around my waist. He's using everything to get me on the ground. I'm not going to let that happen, because he's leaving himself open, and my fist is going to connect with his jaw … right about now.

There's a loud cracking sound before he goes down fast and hard. In fact, I'm pretty sure the guy saw stars. It takes a little over a minute before he blinks his way into consciousness, and it surprises me when he greets me with a smile.

"Congratulations bro," he says, stretching out his arm. "You're a legend."

I like this guy, so I give him a pat on the back, shaking his hand. "Thanks bud. Good job tonight."

"It's an honor."

"You're killing me." I grin. "Hey, take care of yourself out there."

"Yeah, you too." We give our attention to the fans before I make my way over to Pam and Jim. I want to thank them for coming.

"Good job buddy!" a familiar voice shouts from nearby. I turn at the waist, spotting my friend, Logan, who's dressed like he's ready to party.

"Hey, I wasn't sure you were coming."

He shrugs then glances around the coliseum before his eyes land back on me. "You sure you want to leave all this?"

My eyes follow the same direction his just did. "Yeah man. I'm sure."

"Luke!" Pam yells. I reach out to give her a hug, and she gently kisses my cheek, pulling away quickly before getting my sweat on her.

I grin. "Sorry, I'm wet."

"And stinky," she says, holding her nose with her slender fingers.

"That's okay, he can stink," Jim shouts next to me, patting me on the back. "Good fight, son, though I guess you could have stretched it out a bit."

I chuckle. "I was going to wait another round, but he got cocky."

"I saw that." Slipping an arm around Pam's shoulders he asks, "You sure you want to quit?" He watches me intently as though I'll change my mind.

"Why does everyone keep asking that?"

Logan smirks, rocking back and forth on his heels as if he's contemplating an answer.

"You're young," Jim says. "You're not going to miss the fame?" He looks around. "The fans?" His eyes stop on Samantha. "And the women?" He mumbles the last part, and I snicker at the glare he earns from Pam.

"The parties," Logan adds, right as Pam slaps Jim on the back of the head.

I glance at Logan. "It gets old, trust me." Looking at Jim, I add, "And I don't have any problems when it comes to women."

"Enough about the women!" Pam growls. "Why are you encouraging him to fight, Jim? If he wants to lay low, leave him alone about it. Besides, you won't have to worry about him getting hurt."

"That's my cue," Logan interrupts. "I'm going to head out, to *your* party." He emphasizes the word *your*, signaling toward a group of girls who have been staring at us.

"Catch you in a few," I tell him. He waves at the rest of the group then walks away.

"So how long are you two going to be gone?" I ask.

Pam looks at Jim and arches a brow.

"What?" he asks.

"Do you know how long we're going to be gone this time?" she teases. "Because last time you seemed to know, and we ended up staying a lot longer than our original plan."

"Two weeks, but you never know with these things." He scratches his nose as Pam makes faces beside him. "Sometimes it takes longer than expected." Jim likes to go to these marketing conventions, and they usually end up being out of state. Pam thinks they're a waste of time, but she goes with him because he wants her there. He's always looking for ways to make a little more money and have a successful business. A couple years ago they opened their own gym. I thought the idea was perfect and told them I'd help out as soon as I retired. They just didn't expect me to retire this damn soon.

"Does anybody know I'm coming?" I ask them.

Pam places her palm over her forehead and her eyes go wide. "Crap! I didn't get a chance to tell her."

"You better call her," Jim says. My eyes flick back and forth between them.

"I figured it would be good to put the two of you together until we have everything set up for your class." She grabs my shoulders. "Isn't it ironic?"

"Huh?" I tilt my head because I have no idea what she's talking about.

She smiles. "That you and Reese will be working together?"

That name. I know the name. "Wait ... You mean Reese? As in your little neighbor Reese?" My eyebrows shoot up in surprise.

"It hasn't been that long since we've talked about her. She's not little anymore, Luke."

"Yeah, but she's old enough to have a job?"

"Well of course, she's in college now." Pam stares at me like I'm a dumbass.

"She was pretty young the last time I saw her. I guess I have a hard time picturing her as an adult," I reply.

"Well she is, and she's beautiful." The memory of what that prick almost did to her flashes through my mind. By the look on their solemn faces, they were expecting it.

"So she's doing pretty good, huh?" I ask them.

Jim nods. "We told you we'd watch out for her, and we meant it."

"Her mother still lives in the same house. Never remarried. She dates though. There always seems to be a man around. They usually don't stay for long. Then she moves on to the next. When Reese finally got her own apartment, I thought I'd died and gone to heaven. I never liked the burden her mother put on her. It wasn't right. The poor thing grew up too fast." She ruffles my hair. "Sounds like someone else I know."

"That's too bad." I frown.

"She didn't have a choice," Jim says, and I agree with him.

"But she's a fighter," Pam tells me.

"Yes, she is," Jim adds. "Tough little woman."

"Sounds like it." I decide to change the subject 'cause it's getting a little depressing. "So what does she do there, anyway?"

"Oh," Pam smiles. "You're gonna love this. She teaches self-defense classes to young girls," they both say together. "You should see her with them. She's wonderful."

I grin at the thought of that. I couldn't imagine a better job for her. "Perfect ... that's perfect." I scratch the back of my neck, thinking about our working together. "Listen, maybe you shouldn't mention anything to her about who I am. You know? I don't want things to be awkward."

"Why would it be awkward?" Pam asks.

"The situation she was in the last time I saw her? I don't want her to feel embarrassed, that I know ... that I was there that day."

Pam covers her mouth, concerned. "You're right, Luke. I didn't even think about that," she says. But at the same time, you saved her. You saved her from her father, too."

"I just want her to feel like she has some privacy," I say.

"You don't think she'll recognize you?" Jim asks.

I shrug my shoulders. "I doubt it. It's been years. I've put on weight, grown over half a foot. Besides, I don't think I'd recognize her if you hadn't told me. She was what, maybe twelve the last time we saw each other?"

"Something like that," Pam replies. "All right fine. We won't say anything, but when she finds out, and she will, I'm blaming you for making me keep quiet."

"Deal." I grin, reaching out to give her a hug.

"So you ready to go home?" Jim asks.

"More than ready. Even registered for a couple of classes, too."

Pam's eyes twinkle. "You did?"

"Yeah, I figured why not, now that I've got all this time on my hands."

"Go for it. You've got the brain," Jim says, placing his hand on my shoulder. "We're proud of you son."

"Come on baby, just one more time?" she whines, running a nail down my chest, continuing south toward my package. When she reaches the top of my pants I grab her finger, holding it still. "Last time you didn't have any complaints." She frowns, reaching out with her other hand to cup me.

This girl doesn't know when to quit. She's invading my space, and I'm not interested. So I take a step forward and tell her so. "Last time was a mistake." I smirk, leaning down so I'm right in her face. "I'm just not that into you."

She glares at me, disgusted, then flips her hair as she storms away to find her next victim.

"Hey Samantha!" I yell.

She looks over her shoulder and waits.

"Tell Jason I said hey."

She huffs then stumbles off.

Logan chuckles on the couch across from me while he finishes the last of his beer. He's been here a little longer than I have, and he's feeling the effects of the alcohol. "What is wrong with you, man?"

"What do you mean?" I ask, glancing at the familiar blondes he has sitting on each side of him.

"Have you had your eyes checked?"

"What? Samantha? She's engaged." The woman deserves it. She failed to mention that piece of information the night we hooked up.

He covers his mouth. "Awe poor baby. Do you feel used?" The two girls sitting beside him giggle as he flashes a wink.

I place my hand over my heart. "I do, and it hurts."

He quirks an eyebrow and sets his empty cup on the coffee table. "Wait, I'm confused. When has that ever stopped you before?"

"When I happen to know the guy she's engaged to."

"Ouch. That's messed up."

I agree. "He's a pretty solid dude, too."

He nods his head in understanding then squeezes each girl on the thigh. They give each other a look that helps me remember why they're so familiar. "You gonna grab a drink brotha or what?"

"Nah, I'm good."

"That's right, I forgot." Logan rubs his chin. "You quit."

"You quit?" both the blondes ask in sync.

"For now." I run a hand through my hair. "I don't know if it's a permanent thing, but I need a break."

"Congratulations Luke," a guy I don't know says as he walks by with a slap on the back. The music all of the sudden gets louder, and people around us start to dance.

"Thanks man."

"Why are you taking a break?" asks the girl on Logan's left, so he quickly changes the subject to redeem himself.

"Wanna go outside?" He gets up, and I tip my head in the direction of the back, then we squeeze through the growing crowd as Logan chuckles behind me.

"Sorry man," he says, filling his cup at the keg. "I know you like to keep your shit private." His eyes drift to a group of women standing a few feet away, stopping on a tight red mini skirt.

"I told you man, I'm out. Tired of the rumors, done with the drama, ready for the simple life. People are out to destroy you in this business. You never know who you can trust."

I realize I'm wasting my breath when Logan drops his cup to get a peek at the chick's panties. "Are you sure the drama isn't worth it?" He cocks a brow before his eyes meet mine. "Pink lace," he mouths, flashing a smile.

"You're ruthless."

"And you're a saint," he scoffs before gulping down the rest of his beer.

A girl walks up and instantly plants a kiss on my mouth before I have time to see her face. When she walks away she gives me a little wave.

"She's hot."

I agree. She is.

"What? No sex either?" He gives a half smirk.

"I said I was taking a break from alcohol, not taking a vow with the Jonas Brothers."

He chuckles. "Did you see those twins inside? TWINS, Luke."

"Triplets," I reply, then clear my throat. "Yeah, I saw them."

He blinks in disbelief, and I laugh out loud.

"Why is it that you always tap them first? I'm sick and tired of your leftovers." His eyes travel to the chick in the red skirt. "You get a piece of that, too?"

I shake my head no, even though I'm not sure if I have or haven't. I couldn't tell you how many there's been and swear it's not something I'm proud about.

Logan breaks me out of my thoughts. "Truly, I'm shocked. You've actually left one untainted."

"Yeah well, what can I say, I've been a whore. Maybe I should slow down with the ladies, too. I'm pretty sure it's bad for my health."

He grins. "You know what? I think you becoming a monk isn't such a bad idea."

Shortly after, Logan does a keg stand and heads off into the bathroom with some girls. That's when I decide to call it a night. I swear I'm getting too old for this.

Chapter Two

Mumford and Sons blares fiercely through my cell phone, jolting me awake from my past. Blinking my eyes open, I focus on the dated popcorn ceiling, frustrated at the dampness of my clothes. I stretch my arms and legs before I wiggle my fingers and toes, and I'm pleasantly surprised there isn't any soreness. It's a feeling I've come to expect, working as what some may call a punching bag for twelve little pre-teen girls.

As I jump out of bed, I run my fingers through my hair and am sadly disappointed I have to wash it. I was hoping I'd be able to get away with it today; if I'd known I wouldn't, I would have done it last night. Peeling off my sweaty clothes, I toss them in the hamper then twist the broken dial to turn on the water. While I wait for it to heat I glance at my reflection, then tread closer to the mirror to examine my eye. I was supposed to be paying attention to Ally instead of staring at the cocky bastard who distracted me. She got me pretty good, and it's still a little tender, but the bruising isn't as bad as I had expected.

The lights above the mirror begin their usual flicker, and I ignore it as I'm reminded of my father. It's been ten years since the last time I saw him, and though I want to forget, he's always there in my features. The resemblance between us is uncanny, even down to the freckles sprinkled across my nose. Our almond shaped eyes are a darker green, which is a sharp contrast to our olive-colored skin. As far as my mother, nobody would guess we're related. Her natural shade of blonde is the color that women pay for, and her pale blue eyes are nothing like my jade ones. Although I'm much shorter than my father, I've got my mother by at least four inches. She's petite, at just under five-feet tall. Truth be told, we're opposites, in more ways than just the physical, and I'd be lying if I said I wasn't glad about it.

Goosebumps spread all over my flesh as soon as I step into the shower. Under the scalding hot water I rock back and forth, taking in the coconut scent as I scrub and lather my body. There's nothing I find more relaxing, even in the blazing summer heat of Phoenix, Arizona. I set my alarm earlier than I need, and I plan on taking my precious time to enjoy this. Closing my eyes, I work my fingers over my scalp, as memories of the night before flash before me.

"Jim and Pam hired a new guy," Kyle my goofy coworker who usually stays behind the customer service counter, said.

His statement surprised me, so I asked, "Is he a trainer?" Only because I know we could use a couple more.

He shakes his head. "The guy called up and said he's coming in. Said he's an instructor."

"Instructor for what? And how come I'm the last to hear about it?"

He shrugged his shoulders. "Beats me, I just heard thirty minutes ago. He said something about Martial Arts. Self-defense I guess."

That caught my attention. Pulling my hair out of the messy bun I had put it in, I ask, "Did you call Jim and Pam to confirm?" I follow him into the laundry room and watch as he grabs a new batch of clean towels.

"No, but the guy said he's already hired. Said Pam told him she'd call here to fill us in." He dumps the towels out on the counter and starts to fold them, and I reach over to help.

"Is he teaching adults?"

"I really don't know any details." He sets down the towel he's holding and looks at me. "Why don't you call Pam and ask?"

Biting my lip, I hesitate then say, "Do you think that he's taking my place?"

Kyle's eyes go wide, and he chuckles. "Are you kidding me? They love you. Trust me, you'd be the last person they'd replace."

"But why wouldn't they tell me?"

He pulls open the drawer and grabs the schedule. "Tamara and Kelly worked with them last, maybe they know something." Setting the folded towels below the counter he adds, "Who knows, maybe they just forgot?"

"Yeah, you're probably right." Maybe he is right. Maybe it is just my paranoia that has me bothered. But my students are my life. We have a great connection. And I'll be damned if someone comes and takes it all away from me. I narrow my eyes and say, "If any of them call up here, please come find me."

"Will do."

I point at him. "I don't care if you interrupt my class or if you have to get me out of the girls' locker room. I need to find out what's going on."

Tilting his head to the side, he says, "There have been a lot of requests for Martial Arts classes. Maybe he'll teach Jiu-Jitsu. That'd be pretty sweet."

"That would be." I pick up the phone and try Pam. "Does Kelly work today?"

"Nope, just me and you."

"Ugh." I roll my eyes.

"Thanks. I love you, too."

"Stop it. You know what I mean." I hang up the phone a little harder than I should. "She's not answering. I'm freaking out a little."

"Ya think?" He chuckles.

Class is about to begin, and my girls are all lined up side-by-side. They're anxiously waiting to get inside the octagon. I can't help but smile when I spot Ally's sassy hairdo. Her usual long blonde locks are cut into a short bob that accentuates her features. Knowing she needs the attention, I choose to use her for the demonstration in the lesson.

"Now remember, Ally, I'm a professional. You don't need to worry about hurting me. When I'm close enough behind you, I want you to attack me with all you've got." I lean down so that our faces are level. "Do you remember what I showed you last week?"

She gazes at me with her big brown eyes, frowning as she puts on her armor. "Aren't you gonna wear some protection?"

My heart melts at the concern on her face. Ally happens to be my best friend's nine-year-old niece. She also happens to be my favorite student. Her parents decided to enroll her after an incident she had with some girls at school, and I've already seen a difference in her confidence. "The armor's for you kids. I'll be fine."

She doesn't look convinced, but she gets in the proper position anyway, standing in front of me.

"Remember, you can do a lot of damage with your elbow. Aim for my eyes or nose. Pick an area that will give you more time to get away."

She nods her head as I speak from behind her.

"And I know what's coming, so don't worry, I'll block you. Okay?"

"Okay," her muffled voice says through the mask.

"Ready?"

"Ready."

As I creep up from behind she's throwing elbows from her left and then her right. I'm immediately impressed at her defense as I block her with my hands, stepping back to protect my face. "You're doing great Ally! Keep it up!" I yell, and she does exactly as I ask.

A minute later I hear male voices, then shortly after, the girls begin to snicker.

"Good job Ally," I mumble, then, because I'm curious, I glance toward the distraction. I see Kyle standing with a grin on his face. But it's the handsome man beside him that renders me speechless.

He's striking—incredibly so—but familiar, and the way his eyes are on me is a little unnerving. I notice one of his arms is covered in a sleeve of tattoos, and his hair is sticking up in several directions. When I finally meet his gaze, the corner of his mouth curls up into a devious smirk.

Right then it hits me. This man is the new employee, the extremely handsome new employee, who's possibly taking my job. I scowl at him, giving *him the most menacing glare I can muster, then as soon as I turn around, something collides straight into the center of my eye. "Ow!"*

Ally's little elbow gets me full force, and before I realize what I'm doing, I lie flat on my back as all the girls surround me. I have one hand cupping my eye and the other flat on the floor, but the real reason I'm lying here is because I'm humiliated. *Please God, tell me he didn't see it.*

"I'll go get some ice," Taylor yells.

Ally kneels down above my head while Maddy and Rylee sit on each side of me. I squeeze my eyes shut, hoping we no longer have an audience, but I can't bring myself to look.

"I'm so sorry Reese. Are you mad at me?" Ally says, her lip quivering as she starts to cry.

Opening one eye I look at her sweet face. "Shhh ... No Ally, I'm fine. You did great!"

"Next time you should wear protection."

"You're right," I say. "What was I thinking?"

Snapping into the present, I rinse out my hair then turn off the water. Rushing over to my closet, I quickly grab a pink tank and pair it with my favorite denim shorts. I don't have time to style my hair so I throw it up into a messy bun and put on just enough make-up to hide the purple tint of my bruise.

Fifteen minutes before the start of my dreaded statistics class, and I just remembered I forgot to call my mother. She took it pretty hard the day I decided to live on my own, but I couldn't deal with the drama, and I was tired of seeing her cry. You would think she'd learn her lesson after several years with my father, but what I've come to realize is that she's addicted to the abuse.

"Hello," her chipper voice answers on the first ring.

"Mom?"

"Hi baby."

"Hey." I smile. "How is everything? Sorry I didn't call you last night, I got home late."

"Oh," she says, sounding a little too excited. "Would a man have anything to do with that?"

"Nooo." I roll my eyes. "I worked late. It was a long shift."

I hear her huff into the phone, "I wish you would quit that job. The pay is next to nothing, and it takes up all your time. You need to work at a place where you can find somebody."

"There are men that come into the gym, Mother. Plenty, in fact; I just haven't found one I'm interested in."

"How would they notice you anyway? Those clothes do nothing for your figure."

"I work with children!" I argue. "What do you want me to wear?"

"Definitely not what you're wearing."

"Thanks." I frown, wishing I never called her. "You know, you really know how to make me feel shitty."

"What is it baby?" she whines. "Is it that you're not interested in men?"

I blink a couple of times. "Wait a minute … what?"

"Are you?" she hesitates. "Oh God, I'm just going to come out and say it. Are you a lesbian?"

"Excuse me?" I shout because I'm irritated that she's serious. "No, I'm not a lesbian! I'm attracted to guys, and I thought you already knew that!"

"Well, I'm just concerned about why you're not dating. You're young, and it's what young people do," she says it like she's trying to convince me.

"Mom, I don't need a man to make me happy. I'm working two jobs, going to school, and perfectly content being alone." I frown after thinking about the fact that I am indeed alone.

"Sometimes I wonder if I made a mistake back when I let you sign up for those classes." I pull my phone away and glare before bringing it back to my ear.

"Mom, letting me take those classes was probably the best choice you've ever made."

"I really hope so."

Remembering the reason why I called, I change the subject. "I've been meaning to ask, how's Tim treating you these days?"

"Tim? He's wonderful." Her voice gets higher, which is usually what happens when she is nervous.

"Really?"

"Uh huh."

I can tell by the way she says this—she knows I don't believe her. "Does he still call you a whore?"

"Uh ... did I tell you that?" she stutters. "I guess maybe he did say that once or twice." Hell yeah he did, on many occasions, and probably still does. "He has his moods as all men do, and we just need to understand that. We all have our moods, you know?"

"No Mom, I don't, and you deserve better." I wait for her to drop the subject like she always does.

"I love you baby, and I just want you to be happy. Never mind about Tim and me. You need to start thinking about yourself and finding your own man."

"Okay Mom, whatever you say." I sigh. "Are you okay on money? Do you need any?"

"I think we're good, but I'll let you know if we get low." I grind my teeth together when she says the word *we*. I have no problem helping my mother out financially, but when she throws Tim in the mix, I don't trust where it's going.

"Don't be a stranger, baby."

"I won't Mom. I love you."

"Love you too. Bye."

I hang up the phone and toss it into my purse.

Chapter Three

Reese

She's got to be here somewhere. I search the circular room relieved I don't have to suffer through this alone. There's a sudden buzzing against my hip as my phone frantically vibrates inside my purse. I dig around, frustrated, finally finding it in the last pocket. Struggling to get a good grip, it tumbles out of my hand, heading straight toward the floor. "Shoot!" I yell, trying to catch it before the hard surface destroys it. A large hand swoops down to soften the landing.

"Here kid," I hear a charming voice connected to the hand say.

"Thanks," I offer, before looking up to give him a smile. *Even though I don't like the way he emphasized the word, kid.* My eyes fall upon his black chucks then lift to his stylish denim jeans and plain white t-shirt that I notice is fitted perfectly over a pair of broad shoulders and a nicely defined chest. Attached to that chest are two tatted up, muscular arms. I realize I am admiring what I am looking at and may soon forgive him for his earlier comment. As I get to his five o'clock-shadowed jaw line and full lips, it dawns on me that I am studying him in slow motion. *Please God I hope I haven't been here too long.* As soon as I get to his eyes my breath catches in my throat, and I'm no longer breathing.

I didn't get a good look at the guy applying for *my* job last night. I only saw him from a distance. I could tell he was attractive, tall, and built. There is something about his eyes, his messy brown hair, and the way he is looking at me that makes me certain that this is the same guy, and if I am right, then he knows exactly who I am. My heart is pounding fast. I don't know if it's because I am nervous or pissed off.

"How's your eye?" he says in a soft, sincere voice.

Blinking out of my shock, I reach up to touch my face. "Oh … umm … it's fine. I'm fine," I stutter.

"You sure? She got you pretty good. Did you ice it?" *Why is he looking at me like that?*

I nod as his eyes look down at my phone that happens to be vibrating in my hand. Following his gaze, I read the text.

CLOSE YOUR MOUTH! YOU'RE DROOLING! LOL! WHO IS THAT? I'M DIRECTLY ACROSS FROM YOU.

I snap my head up to find Gia smirking at me, like I had some secret she couldn't wait to hear. Shoving my phone in my purse, I quickly walk across the room and take the spot next to her.

Gia's light brown, curly hair spills just past her shoulders, her big blue eyes usually melt a man's heart within seconds, not to mention her petite little frame. She's sweet, yet confident, and like my mom, is always pushing me to date. I know what she is up to. I can read her thoughts before she even speaks, which seems to be a common thing in our relationship.

"Who the *heck* is that?" she mumbles, raising her eyebrows, looking down at her desk. I can tell she's trying to keep him from reading her lips.

Trying not to be obvious, I slowly glance his way. Unfortunately, it doesn't work since he is staring directly at me. He isn't smiling or frowning. He looks so ... *worried* ... if that makes any sense. *Why in the world is he still looking at me like that?*

Not wanting him to read my lips, I glance at Gia from the side with my head facing down and quietly explain the gym incident. "He is the reason for this!" I hiss, pointing directly at my black eye.

She chuckles. "Come on, it's not his fault he's good looking."

I roll my eyes. "That is not why I got distracted. It's the way he was watching me. I think he might be taking my job, and he feels bad about it or something."

Gia shakes her head. "You're not going to lose your job. They love you. I'm sure there's another reason he's got his eyes on you." She gives me a little kick in the shin. "Maybe he thinks you're hot?"

I rub my leg and look her directly in the eyes this time, growling. "I know that look Gia, and this definitely is not *The Look*."

"Don't growl at me," she says, rolling her eyes. "All I'm saying is, he keeps staring at you, and it's definitely not a stare that says, 'Hey baby, I'm taking your job, and I feel real bad about it.'"

"Maybe he's looking at you."

She twirls her already curly hair around her finger. "Nope. Definitely looking at you."

"Regardless of who he's looking at, it doesn't matter. I don't like him."

She presses her glossy lips into a tight line and glares at me—a look I've seen many times before. "Stop looking for flaws in every single man you meet. You're never going to find Mr. Perfect. Mr. Perfect doesn't exist."

"You don't need to convince me." She just doesn't get it. I'm not interested in dating. Period. "I never said I was looking."

"You know you're terrible, right?"

The conversation ends when Professor Hornsby begins role call.

"Reese Johnson."

"Here," I say quickly, meeting the curious eyes of the handsome male across the way. "If he wants a staring contest I'll give him a staring contest," I mutter. "I do not intimidate easily." Placing the tip of my pen in my mouth I match his stare and hear Gia giggle under her breath beside me. I assume he's onto my game when a slow crooked smile spreads across his lips. *Oh, he's good ... He's real good.* I raise my eyebrows, throwing back my wickedest grin before my cheeks redden and betray me. *What's so funny, you big cocky jerk?* I'm angry and somewhat affected by the confidence radiating off his face. He leans back in his chair, now grinning from ear to ear, his hand moves in circles around his mouth. *Is he asking if I enjoy his smile? What's that supposed to mean?*

Gia taps my arm with her pen. "Does that mean he wants a kiss?"

"I have no idea," I mumble back, desperate to win our contest.

"Oh my gosh!" Gia squeals, yanking on my arm.

"Not right now. I can't let him win this."

"Yes, right now! Reese, look at me!" She jerks me harder, trying to get my attention, but I shake my head no, refusing to look away from his annoying, confident face.

"Here," comes out of his mouth after the professor calls out a name. I'm too focused on our contest to hear what it is.

"Reese, look at me! You have … look at me!"

"What the heck, Gia!" I say, finally snapping my head in her direction. "Why are you looking at me like that?"

"Go to the bathroom now!"

"What?" I ask, confused by the horrified look on her face.

"There is ink all over your mouth," she says, trying her best to keep from laughing.

"No," I whisper back, barely able to catch my breath. I look down at my pen and gasp. There is ink all over my fingers. Then it dawns on me. *He was trying to tell me. He was laughing at me.* Looking back over at Gia, I cover my face. "You have got to be kidding me," I mumble. "Is it bad?"

"Terrible," she says, biting back another laugh. Could I really blame her? I probably look like a complete idiot. "Don't hate me for laughing," she snorts. "I'm really trying not to."

I won't even look his direction. I can't. "I've got to get out of here."

"Go home. I'll take notes." I nod my head, still covering my mouth, and quickly bolt out of the classroom without any intention of returning for the rest of the day.

"What did you say?" I ask Gia over the phone.

"His name, Luke Ryann? What? You didn't hear it during your staring contest?" She giggles.

"Ugh, I'm mortified."

"Bet you guys are going to hook up. Best friends know these kind of things."

I open my mouth, then shut it, then open it again. "I said I'm not interested. Would you stop trying to hook me up?"

"Whatever you say."

Tapping my finger to my now sensitive lips, I tell her, "I need to talk to Pam, and find out what's going on. If he's not taking my job then maybe I'll let him live."

"That's so kind of you," she teases.

"Enough about Luke. Are you still coming over? We need to study."

"Yep. I'm on my way."

Biting my nails, I look over at Gia and can tell she's just as confused as I am. "So you don't remember what he said about the differences?"

She tilts her head to the side. "Differences?"

"You know. Between a Z-score and a T-score?"

Scrunching her eyebrows together, she taps her pen along her notebook. "I thought I wrote it down, but my notes are a little confusing." I glance at the clock resting on my end table, noticing I've got forty-five minutes to get ready. "Do you have plans tonight?" she asks, her voice sounding a little disappointed.

"I work at Chili's at two o'clock."

She gets up off the floor and picks up her books. "That sucks. I wish you didn't have to work so much."

I grab a throw pillow from the couch and plop it into my lap. "It's fine. I'm gonna cut back my hours soon, maybe just keep the job at the gym."

Gia comes from a long line of money. Her parents have always paid for everything she wants and needs. Even though she knows I come from the opposite side of the tracks, she has a hard time watching me work as much as I do. To me, it's not a big deal. To her, well ... she was raised to believe money grows on trees.

"You know I can always help." I shake my head in response. She always offers me money, her parents' money, and there is no way I would ever feel comfortable accepting it.

"Thanks Gia, but I'm not going to take your daddy's money."

She throws her hands on her hips in her best attempt to give me attitude. "If my daddy gives me money, it then becomes my money. Therefore, you wouldn't be taking my daddy's money; you'd be taking mine."

"If you say so." I roll my eyes as she swats me on the butt.

"Fine, work your little heart out, but we need a girls' night out. At least let me pay for that."

"You're right. We definitely do, but I can pay for myself."

She growls and gives me a tight hug. "You're the most stubborn person I know."

"I love you," I say in a singsong voice.

"Have a good shift," she sings back before shutting the door behind her.

I take a quick shower, attempt to cover up my black eye, and scarf down a turkey sandwich before checking on my mom.

"Hey it's me, getting ready for work, and just thought I'd check in. Call me if you need anything … money or whatever. I have my cell. Love you, bye."

After brushing my teeth, I take a swig of mouthwash and head out the front door, toward my little white Civic.

"Hey Reese." I see the cute little blonde boy that lives across the way heading toward me.

"Hey Johnny." I smile, reaching out to pat him on the top of his head.

Another little boy I don't recognize runs over from the same apartment. "Hi," he says, smiling. He turns to Johnny, quietly mumbling something, and I notice he's missing a front tooth.

"Told you," Johnny says to the boy, as they smile and snicker together.

I look at him, confused. "Told him what?"

Johnny blushes. "That you're hot."

I gasp. "Johnny! You're too young to be talking like that."

He said you smell good, too," the other boy says, smiling wide and flashing his missing tooth.

"He did, huh?" I grin. "What's your name, kiddo?"

"Caleb."

"Well hello, Caleb. I'm Reese," I say, leaning over to shake his hand. He giggles while we shake, and I watch Johnny's face turn beet red. "Listen boys, I need to go to work, but it's been fun talking to you."

"It sure has," Johnny says back, and Caleb laughs with him.

"Okay funny guy," I say to Johnny. "How old are you again?"

Both boys say, "Eight," at the same time.

"Wow. That's really getting up there." They nod their heads in agreement.

"You know what?"

"What?" Caleb asks.

I place my hands on my hips. "You two are good looking boys. I bet your pick up lines will work really well on a pretty little girl your own age."

They both look at each other like they're thinking about it. "You do?" Johnny finally asks.

"Yeah. You should try it."

Johnny looks at Caleb and shrugs his shoulders. "Okay."

"Caleb loves Melody," Johnny blurts out, and now its Caleb's face that turns red. I think about the brunette little girl I saw Johnny running around with the other day.

"Is that the girl I saw you playing with the other day? The one with the long brown hair, wearing that pretty sundress?"

"Probably," Johnny mumbles. "But Caleb is the one that loves her. Not me."

Caleb looks mortified, and I completely know the feeling. So I place a hand on his shoulder and whisper, "Don't be embarrassed. I won't tell." I give him a wink. "You should try and use your swagger on her. I bet she likes you, too."

He smiles at me before saying, "Okay, I'll do it." The look of determination on his face is adorable.

"Let me know how it goes when you do."

"I will," he says seriously, and suddenly I feel like a matchmaker.

"See you later boys," I say, waving.

Boys will be boys.

Chapter Four

"You're in cocktail tonight," Jessica, the hostess, says, standing at the podium right in front of the entrance. This is where they've put me for the past couple months, sharing tables with my handsome friend, Robert. He trained me as a waitress when I first got hired and we've been close ever since.

"Cool." I smile, happy with where they put me. "Is Robert working?"

"Yeah, he's around here somewhere." She turns at the waist, glancing behind her before saying under her breath, "looking about as fine as he possibly can." She runs her fingers through her hair like she's looking for split ends.

"Doesn't he always?" I ask, shaking my head, not waiting for a response as I head toward the kitchen. I reach the front line and see Robert leaning against it, finishing up a basket full of chips. "There he is." I smile, stretching my arms out to give him a hug.

"Hey gorgeous." He squeezes me tightly, nuzzling my neck before letting go. "Mmm, you smell good."

"You smell pretty good yourself."

"You know it." His blue eyes sparkle as he gives me a wide smile, flashing celebrity white teeth.

I stare at him for a minute, taking in the perfect features of his face then ask, "Can you tell me why it is that all the good guys are gay?"

He laughs, placing his hands on my shoulders. "What ever do you mean?"

"I'm serious! You're good looking, smart, sweet—you're just an all around great guy."

"Stop it! You're making me blush," he teases.

"You know it's true." I playfully swat him on the hip. "You working another double today?"

"Yeah, I didn't make anything during the lunch shift."

"I'm sorry," I say, sticking my bottom lip out in a pout. "They have you in cocktail, right?"

"You and me both, sister."

A few hours roll by, and Robert and I are slammed with customers. Most of my tables are filled with rowdy college boys who are getting drunker and drunker by the minute. An impatient customer with a Packers hat and jacked up teeth shouts for another round of beer. Judging by the creepy looks I've been getting the past hour—the kind that make my skin crawl—I'm beginning to think he's reached his limit. I glance at Robert's tables to see if he could use my help and spot a pretty blonde girl, probably close to my age, sitting at a small booth in the corner. She has the cutest hairstyle I've ever seen, so I head over to ask her where she gets it done. I've always been in to trendy hair, especially since I'm unhappy with my own. "I love your hair," I say enthusiastically, leaning my hip against the wall, taking a quick break.

She looks up at me with a genuine smile, and her pretty eyes twinkle. "Thank you. That's so sweet," she says, gently placing her hand on my arm.

"Has your server greeted you yet?" She's about to answer before she glances at the door and waves. My eyes follow the direction of her gaze, and good Lord Almighty, I'm staring directly into the eyes of Luke Ryann—the guy from my class, the guy from the gym, and the guy who all of the sudden keeps popping into my life. I blink a couple times out of confusion and feel like a complete idiot. Once again I am unable to speak, and my mouth is most likely open. Luke looks a little different. His five o'clock shadow is gone. He's dressed in a white polo shirt and dark gray shorts. Unfortunately, he looks just as sexy as he did before, sort of like a bad boy getting all cleaned up for a special occasion. Lucky for me, he looks just as confused as me.

"Hi," he says. The corner of his mouth turns up while his eyes slowly roam over my face. Standing speechless, I feel it flush, as the scent of soap and light cologne consumes me. Then the strangest thing happens. It's as if I've seen this play out before. Something about his scent, and the look in his eyes brings a sense of déjà vu. I can't seem to place it, but it's so familiar that I can't be imagining it.

Not only that, but his proximity is doing strange things to my body—things that make my skin tingle and my heart beat faster than it should.

Once I get my brain working, I try my best to play it cool. Clearing my throat, I say, "Do I know you?" Of course I know him. At least, I've already met him. But he doesn't need to know that I remember who he is. *He* slides into the seat across from his date, and I can tell he's clearly amused.

Without taking his eyes off me, he responds, "Lauren, this is Reese; Reese; this is Lauren. She and I work together at the gym." *Work together? Okay, maybe he's not taking my job.*

Flashing a wide smile that stretches across her face, she reaches out to shake my hand. "Nice to meet you, Reese. Wow, what a small world."

I smile back at her. "Yeah, it is." I glance at Luke. "I'm sorry, what was your name again? My memory's not that great," I say in my most sincere voice.

"Luke. Luke Ryann." He reaches out to shake my hand, and I hesitate before finally shaking it.

"It's nice to officially meet you, Luke." Our hands linger a little before I let go when an impatient customer interrupts me, demanding I get him another beer. I hold up my finger in his direction. "I'll be right there." I look back at Luke and Lauren. "I better get back to my tables, but I can take your order if you're ready."

"Go ahead and take care of them first if you need to. It's not a problem," Lauren says, flicking her eyes in the direction of the four guys at the next table. The guy with the jacked up teeth is holding up his empty beer mug, waving his Packers hat back and forth to get my attention.

"Don't worry about it. Everyone kind of came in at once so I'm trying to help my friend out. Robert is actually your server. You guys will love him." I grab my notepad and pen, pulling the cap off with my teeth.

"Careful with that pen now." I look up at Luke, who teasingly gives me a wicked grin. Once again I blush, mortified by the memories of what happened at school.

"Haha, very funny," I say, raising an eyebrow. Lauren looks back and forth between us.

"Am I missing something?" She furrows her brows in confusion. I silently pray Luke doesn't tell her. Today's incident gave me enough embarrassment to last a lifetime.

"It's nothing," he says, shaking his head, still grinning. "You had to be there."

"Gotcha," she says, before closing the menu to put it away.

After Luke and Lauren place their orders I run over to check on the rest of my tables, dropping another Bud Light to the Packers guy at table 101. "What kind of jeans are those?" the guy asks.

"Excuse me?"

He makes a circle motion with his finger and says, "Turn around and let me see your pockets." He grins, and I'm a little grossed out by his abnormally yellow teeth.

"They're nothing special," I say, tilting my head. "I'm sorry, I'm a little confused by what you're asking me."

"Well, let me clarify then. I want to get a good, long look at your ass," he slurs as his hooded eyes begin to undress me.

My blood boils at the way his stare is making me feel, and I have a hard time keeping my composure. I mentally prepare to lean in close and make my point clear. "That was your one chance," I say, narrowing my eyes, looking straight into his.

I turn around and walk away, hearing one of his friends ask, "What'd she say?"

Then another male voice says, "Dude, I think I know her from somewhere."

"Would you rather the raven-haired guy with the black button down shirt at table 101, or the guy sitting with the girl at 117?" Robert asks as I watch him ring up an order on the computer. I glance at table 101, which is my high-top filled with the belligerents. The guy with the button down shirt is the most attractive in the group, but there's no comparison to the handsome man at 117, who just so happens to be Luke.

"Who would you pick?" I ask him.

"You first."

"No, you first."

"There's no question," he grins. "Definitely the GQ at 117." Without being obvious, I glance over at Luke while he intently listens to Lauren engage him in conversation. They're not holding hands, and their body language wouldn't tell you whether they're romantically involved. Before I tell Robert I agree, the Packers guy shouts for me.

"Hey pretty little thing, I need another beer!" He has that look on his face people get when they're really drunk and their eyes can't focus. I turn to Robert and mumble through my teeth.

"That guy seriously has a death wish." I try to avoid eye contact with the creep and look at his friends as I walk back to their table.

"Do you need me to call a cab?" I ask, focusing my attention on everyone but the Packers guy.

His friend sitting to the left with the button down shirt says, "I'm drivin'." Placing one hand on his stomach and stretching out his other arm, a lazy grin appears on his face. The other two men are engaged in a conversation about *hos* and *clubbin'*. I glance at his drink, remembering he switched to water about an hour ago.

"And you're okay to drive?" I ask, placing my hands on my hips.

His grin widens, and he nods his head before saying, "Hey, you work at the gym, right?"

Someone nudges me in the shoulder just as I'm about to answer, and Robert whispers in my ear, "You have a new table. I already took his drink order." I've been so distracted by these jerks that I didn't even notice the man at the small booth behind me.

"Thanks babe," I say, following him to the back of the bar.

"No problem. Just so you know, I'm cut. His eyes flick over to my obnoxious table. "You going to be okay?"

As if his ears were ringing, the Packers guy yells, "Where's my beer?"

I roll my eyes and chuckle, looking at Robert. "Seriously, I've been gone for five seconds! If I get arrested for assault tonight, will you bail me out?"

He laughs. "Not only would I bail you out, I will pay you to rough up Packers fan over there. He's just nasty."

"Trust me. I'm about to."

I head over to the booth, placing a napkin and silverware on the table before my eyes meet a familiar face, and my heart comes to a complete stop. My father sits before me, looking very much like I remember. The look on his face is pained, and his green eyes look directly into mine. *This cannot be happening. Can this night get any worse?* He slowly stands up, reaching his arms out to embrace me, but I stay frozen with my arms at my sides while he holds me. I look around the room, confused about why he's here and rest my eyes on Luke as he stares back at me in what seems to be… understanding. *Please God let this be a dream.* Seconds later, my father speaks.

"Reese," is all he says.

"What are you doing here?" I ask, gritting my teeth. He closes his eyes, running a hand through his dark hair.

"You won't answer my letters; you haven't returned any of my calls."

"So you show up at my place of work?" I hiss. He fidgets with the knife and fork lying on top of the tiled table.

"I know you're upset, and I'm sorry, but I don't know how else to reach you." He glances at the occupied tables around us before looking back at me. "Have you read any of my letters?"

"No," I growl. "I don't want you in my life. Things have been going just fine without you, and I don't need you coming back around to screw it up."

"Your mom has forgiven me. I'm a changed man, Reese."

"That says a lot. Mom forgives everyone; she's no example," I spit. He nods his head in agreement, keeping his eyes aimed on the floor.

"That may be true ... she's a sick woman, Reese, and I was a sick man when I hurt both of you. I'm not that man anymore. I quit drinking. I go to church." He stares down at his hands that are resting on the table. "I just want to be a father to you. The father that I never was, the father I need to be." He lifts his head, his eyes pleading with me. I hold back tears as we stare at each other, not wanting to give in to the lies. He pulls out his wallet and drops a hundred dollar bill on the table, along with a business card. "I'll leave now since you don't want me here."

"I don't want your money," I say quietly, but he ignores me and stands up before speaking again. He glances over my shoulder toward Luke and gives a slight nod. He must have seen him watching us. I hate that this is happening in public, in front of all these people. It was a stupid thing for him to do.

"Is everything okay?" Bill, my manager walks up and asks. I consider having my father thrown out, not that Bill would do it, but the thought did cross my mind.

"We're fine," my father says. "I'm her father."

"He was just leaving," I interrupt.

My manager reaches out his hand. "Bill." He smiles. "I'm her manager. Nice to meet you." I watch my father shake his hand, desperately wanting him to leave.

"Well, I won't keep you, since you have somewhere you need to be," Bill says. I speak before my father can get a word in.

"Thanks Bill. He was supposed to leave twenty minutes ago." My father keeps his face blank and thankfully doesn't argue.

After Bill walks away, leaving me with my father, it feels as though we are the only ones left in the room. "I'll keep writing," he hesitates, "I know I don't deserve it, but I hope that one day you'll find it in your heart to forgive me." I don't know what to say. I don't know how to respond. So all I do is watch him until he turns around and walks out the door.

Chapter Five

Reese

I squeeze my eyes shut, trying to keep the tears at bay before heading toward the back of the bar to start on my side work.

"You okay?" Luke asks softly.

I turn in his direction and find him sitting alone. He is chewing on a straw like a bad habit and tapping his foot nervously. I don't know if Lauren left or if she fell into some trouble in the bathroom, and aside from them, the guys at table 101 are the only people left in the bar.

Finally I say, "Yeah, I'm fine."

"Reese, that's your name, right?" The Packers guy slurs, waving his hand again to get my attention. He's probably going to ask for another beer. I quietly curse him and hesitantly walk to their table.

"That's my name," I say with a fake smile, sticking my hands in the pockets of my apron.

"You don't like me much. Do you Reese?" He smiles, and it's definitely a smile that makes me feel dirty.

"Do you want the truth?" I ask, irritated.

"That's okay, I like a challenge. You don't have to like me," he says slowly. "Are you busy?" His friends chuckle as they watch his eyes roam over my entire body.

"I'm just closing up my tables." I raise my arm to look at my watch. "We close at eleven. Oh wow, I guess we're already past that."

"What time do you get off?" He glances sideways at his friends, and they all continue to laugh as if they have some inside joke. I take a quick peek in Luke's direction and notice the mangled straw that he's destroyed with his teeth. His eyes are staring daggers straight into Packers guy's head.

"If I knew what time I was getting off, I definitely wouldn't be telling you," I say, losing my patience.

"Why don't you go find out real quick," he slurs, then reaches out and runs his fingers down my arm. That's when I snap.

"Get your hands off her," Luke says flatly. His voice startles me, since he's unexpectedly standing right beside me.

"Who are you?" the drunk guy growls, his friends are all wide-eyed and freaked out.

"Sorry man, we didn't know," the guy with the button down shirt says to Luke.

"Didn't know what?" I ask, clearly annoyed that Luke didn't let me fight my own battle.

"You're Luke Ryann," one of the other guys says. "We didn't want to bother you earlier, but we recognized you when you were sitting over there with your girl." I'm confused as to why these guys are looking at him as though he's a legend, and for some reason, it pisses me off.

Luke doesn't even smile. He doesn't even acknowledge anything they've said. He just stands there with his fists clenched, staring at them in a way that should make them want to run for the hills. Finally he opens his mouth, "You owe her an apology, and then you need to leave."

I place my hand on his arm, but he doesn't break the stare he has on the pervert. "Seriously, Luke. Thank you, but I got this."

The Packers guy begins to speak when his friends get up, trying to silence him as they quickly pull him toward the exit.

"Hey Reese," the guy yells.

"Shut up dude," they tell him, pulling him harder. "You're gonna get your ass kicked."

They're frantically shoving him out the door when I hear him slur, "You said she works at your gym, right?" The door slams shut, and I sigh in relief that they are finally gone. I turn to face Luke.

"I don't trust those guys." He presses his lips in a tight line and furrows his brow like he's deep in thought. "What time do you get off?"

"Not until I'm checked out with my manager. Why?" He runs a hand through his hair, leaving a thick chunk of it sticking up. He has the *I just got out of bed look*, which he happens to wear very well.

"I told Lauren to go home. I'll wait for you to finish then follow you to your place."

"Excuse me?" I ask, surprised, not rudely … just surprised.

"Where do you live?"

"Down the street—Citrus Grove Apartments. You don't need to follow me."

"I said I'm following you home. I don't trust those punks," he says flatly.

"Trust me. I'll be fine."

He snorts. "You didn't hear what was said when you walked into the kitchen."

I place my hands on my hips. "Look, I'm flattered that you barely know me, and you're already concerned with my safety. It's sweet… but have you forgotten that I am a self-defense instructor?" I bat my eyelashes and give him a teasing smile. His piercing brown eyes go from concern to amusement.

"No offense, princess, but your self-defense skills won't protect you from being gang-raped by a bunch of drunk guys." He waves me off, as if my previous comment was a joke. That's when I get offended. He didn't even allow me to defend myself earlier, and now I know it's because he thinks I'm weak, which makes me want to choke him. Literally.

"How kind of you to devalue something that I have put my heart and soul into for half of my life." I point my finger at him. "You don't even know me." He rolls his eyes and sighs in frustration.

"That isn't what I meant … what you do is great. But be rational. No matter how much training you've had, it's unrealistic to believe you would be able to get away from four guys." His voice is gentle and his eyes almost pleading. "Hell, I'm a former MMA fighter, have won several titles, and even I probably couldn't come out ahead if they attacked me." I bite my lip as I think about what he said, coming to the conclusion that he's probably right.

"Is that why those guys freaked out? Because they know who you are?"

"Probably. What does that matter?"

"Do you use that face on all the girls?" I ask him. Because the look on his face is part of the reason I'm giving in.

"What?" he asks, genuinely confused.

"Forget it. Okay, you can follow me home." In a way, I'm a little relieved, but there's no way I'd admit that to him.

After checking out with my manager, I see Luke standing in the parking lot next to a shiny black Harley. He's holding a helmet under his arm with a look on his face that spells TROUBLE in giant capital letters. Honestly, the guy is so attractive it's beginning to hurt my eyes. I force myself to look away before I climb in my car and roll down the window. "Do you know where Citrus Grove Apartments are?" He nods his head then slips on his helmet.

It only takes a few minutes to get to my apartment complex, and I pull into my regular spot. I glance over toward Luke and see him parking his Harley nearby. *What on Earth is he doing?* "I can take it from here," I tell him.

"No you don't. I'm walking you to your door," he says, following closely behind me. We walk the rest of the way in silence until I turn around to thank him.

"Thanks for taking time out of your night to follow me home." My breathing is weird, my hands are shaky, and I'm terrified he'll hear my pounding heartbeat.

"Anytime," he says. I turn around, fumbling through my purse for my keys when he places a hand on my shoulder. "Reese."

I turn and look at him, waiting, as his eyes gently scan my face with concern. He has the most beautiful eyes I've ever seen. They are light brown with swirling flecks of amber and gold. His lips are full, and I notice a small scar below his lower lip where he might have had a piercing. His voice comes out softly when he speaks.

"I want you to call me if you run into trouble. Give me your number, and I'll text you."

"Okay," I say, my voice cracking when I answer, and I watch as he saves my number to his phone. Tucking my hair behind my ear, I clear my throat. "Listen, I'm a little confused as to why you're so concerned with my safety? I'm a big girl. I've been living on my own for a while." I place my hand on his shoulder just as he did to me, and notice him looking at the scar above my eye. *One of the scars my father gave me.*

He smirks. "I worry about you kid."

"Why? You don't even know me?"

The corner of his mouth tilts up. "Whatever you say princess." I don't respond and watch him turn around and head back in the direction of parking lot.

"Bye," I shout, confused by his strange behavior.

"See you tomorrow, Reese!" He yells without looking back.

I lie in bed thinking of my father. After spending time in prison for the assault on my mother, it took years before we heard from him. In fact, he didn't start writing the letters until two years ago. The first time my mother told me about the letters, I asked her to burn them. She said she had forgiven him, but I hadn't ... and still don't.

I think my father blamed us for the reason he lost his job. He was a good cop, but a lousy husband and father. He wouldn't accept responsibility for what he did, so he left us. We never got a phone call from prison, and he never contacted us when he was released—two years ago—when it all changed. He called my mother and apologized. He tried to apologize to me, but I refused to speak to him. That's when the letters started coming, nearly everyday. I told my mom I wanted nothing to do with him. But tonight, when I looked into his eyes, they were sad, almost remorseful. I wasn't ready to hear what he had to say, but I could see it on his face. He was sorry.

Closing my eyes, I begin to drift off to sleep when the chirp of my cell phone startles me. I pick it up and see a text from a number I don't recognize. It says, "Good night princess."

I smile and force myself not to text him back as I close my eyes and whisper, "Good night, Luke."

Chapter Six

*The hair stands up on the back of my neck, and chills run all over my body
when I hear the pleading sounds that I know are coming from my mother. I rest
an ear against my bedroom door, nervously waiting for silence. As I creep my
way out of the room then down the dark and narrow hall, I slowly peek my head
around the corner. My father is lying on the living room floor, and my mother is
squirming underneath him. When I'm close enough to see the fearful expression
on her face, I have no doubt that she is in danger. His left hand is pressed
against her mouth, and his right hand is tightly wrapped around her throat.
Terrified for my mother's life, I stumble back to my room and stare out my
window, desperately waiting for the teenage boy.*

I feel intense rage pour out of me as I take out my aggression
on the heavy bag. Between the visit from my father, and the
nightmares of my past, I've had just about as much as I can handle.
Stepping back, I gaze at my reflection, noticing the effects from my
recent lack of sleep. I pull off the gloves and wipe the sweat from
my eyes, jolting to a stop as I tread toward the locker room.

On the other side of the wall, I hear two men engaged in conversation. It doesn't take long for me to recognize the voices belong to Luke and Kyle. Normally I wouldn't snoop like this, but I'm convinced I just heard them say my name. So I crouch behind the wall like the awesome person that I am and try to listen.

"Why? You got a thing for her?" There's a smile in Kyle's tone.

Luke's reply is clipped when he grumbles, "No man. I don't."

I roll my eyes.

"It's okay, man, I'm not going to say anything."

Luke chuckles, but it sounds a little forced. "No Really. Last night there were some guys giving her a hard time. I didn't see her car. I got worried." *That's because I walked.*

"Uh huh, well, just so you know..." I press my ear against the wall when Kyle gets quieter.

"She's a man-hater." He chuckles softly. "The woman's got Daddy issues."

What? Who in the hell told him that? I frown.

"Yeah, well maybe she has her reasons." *Damn straight I do.*

"I guess."

"And just so we're clear, I don't look at her like that ... she's not my type."

That earns a roar out of Kyle, "Yeah dude. She's not my type either."

"You know what I mean," Luke stutters. "She's just a kid. Come on. What kind of guy do you take me for?"

I can't take another word out of his mouth. In fact, I'm speechless. Actually, I'm a lot of things. *A kid? Not his type? Who does he think he is?*

I stand up tall and pat down my hair before gliding past the desk, heading straight to the locker room. They instantly stop talking so I turn my head nonchalantly, show them my fakest smile, and say, "Hi guys."

Kyle quickly clears his throat as Luke strides over and pulls me aside. "What?" I ask sheepishly, forcing myself to look at him. Damn him! How can someone look so good in a flipping wife beater and plain old track pants?

"Why didn't you text me back?" he asks. His scent intoxicates me. I almost forget that I'm pissed and deeply offended.

"I was asleep by the time you sent it," I lie. I don't want to tell him that it took all my willpower not to text him back.

He glances toward the parking lot then drops his gaze on me. "Where's your car?"

"I live right down the street. Remember?" Shrugging, I add, "I walked."

"In this heat?" He grins. "Are you crazy?"

"It's good exercise." *Now stop looking at me that way because I'm supposed to be angry with you.*

"Okay." He slowly nods his head. "I can respect that."

"Good." I smile, pointing toward the locker room. "Are we done? I need to clean up."

"Uh, sure." His eyebrows scrunch together. "Knock yourself out, *kid.*"

"Thanks," I spit. *Really? Did he really just say that?* I burst into the locker room, quickly rushing through my shower, hoping I'll have enough time to call Gia. My pride has been ripped into shreds, and I need some encouragement, but the locker room's filling up fast and I'd like a little privacy. After changing into my clothes I grab my phone and walk over to the break room, relieved when I find it empty, so I hurry up and call.

"Hello," she answers on the first ring.

"Thank God, you answered. You have no idea what I've been through." I run her through the events of the night before, thankful I have another woman to talk to. I tell her about my father, Luke and Lauren, and the creepy guys at table 101. I tell her about Luke following me home, my lack of sleep, and psychotic beating on the punching bag. When I'm finally done she stays silent for what seems like an eternity.

"Hello," I say, hoping I didn't lose her.

"Hahahahaha."

I pull the phone away from my ear. "What's so funny? This is serious!" I can't believe she's actually laughing right now.

"I'm sorry, it's just that, I've never heard you so freaked out over a guy." She's laughing so hard I can barely understand her. "I'm kind of in shock," she continues.

"Did you hear anything else that I said? C'mon Gia, my kids are going to be here any minute. I'm stressing out!"

"You're right. I'm sorry. I heard you." She tries to contain herself, taking on a more serious tone. "Those guys sound pretty scary, and they know you work at the gym? Like which gym?"

"The guy said he recognized me from the gym."

"Just be careful. Make sure you have someone walk you to your car when you leave."

I decide not to mention that I walked today. "Okay."

"I'm sorry I laughed at you earlier," she says gently.

"I'll get over it. You always find something to laugh at me about."

"What can I say? You're funny. Anyway, tell me what happened with your father. How do you feel about it?"

I think of his pained expression. "To be honest, I don't know. He looked ... sorry. Regretful even."

"That's good, Reese. He should be sorry. Who knows, maybe when you're ready, you can talk?"

I had a feeling she would say that, but I'm not ready to talk. "I don't think so." I say, watching a fly land on the wall before I lift up my foot and try to smash it.

"Give it some time. You might change your mind?"

"Yeah maybe." I bite my lip in thought. "But, I doubt it."

"So Luke followed you home, huh?" she asks, changing the subject.

"Yep." I hesitate. "And I haven't even told you the rest of the story."

"Really," she coos. "Do tell."

So I run her through this morning's events, and the conversation I overheard between Luke and Kyle. "How old do you think he is?" I ask her.

"Anywhere between twenty-five and thirty would be my guess."

"Yeah, mine too. What's his deal, saying I'm just a kid?"

"I don't know. It's weird."

"I wonder if it's why he's so protective? He thinks I'm a child."

She chuckles. "So tell him how old you are."

I bite my nails, mumbling, "How am I supposed to do that? Hey Luke, guess how old I am?"

"I don't know, figure it out."

"You're a big help." I glance at the clock. "I gotta go; my students are probably waiting."

"Okay, just keep me posted, and good luck!"

I spin around and squeal at finding Luke standing right behind me. His sparkling eyes and prominent dimples are all the confirmation I need to know that he heard. *This CANNOT be happening!*

"I'm sorry," he says, beaming. "Am I interrupting something?" He leans against the wall confidently, with his muscled arms folded at his chest.

"I... I..." For some reason my mouth momentarily stops working.

His eyes light up in amusement. "You were saying?"

Heat burns in my cheeks, running all the way down my neck. I want to disappear and never come back. I can't muster a word with my mouth hanging open. It's that stupid *deer in the headlights* look I always seem to have whenever I'm around him. The man gets under my skin, and I don't like him, and now that my embarrassment is turning to anger, I'm going to tell him so.

"Get over yourself! I wasn't spying on you," I hiss. "I was headed to the locker room and heard my name. I didn't hear much except for the fact that you said …" Ticking off on my fingers, "I'm not your type, and oh yeah, I'm just a kid. Whatever that means?" I look at him like that statement's ridiculous, stepping close enough to poke him in the chest. "Who do you think you are?" He cocks a brow, and I keep going. "You don't know me. You walk in here thinking you're *God's gift to all* and expect me to bow at your feet and do whatever you say."

He smiles, actually smiles at me, which makes me angrier. "I have news for you, buddy!" I poke him harder. "I'm not one of those women. I'm not going to do what you say, and I don't need you to do me any favors. I am twenty years old. I'm not a child, and I don't appreciate being treated like one." A look of surprise flashes in his eyes as he stops the finger that's poking him to hold it. He smells divine, and he looks like he just walked off an Armani poster. Damn, I hate him for it.

He presses his lips together tightly. "I thought you were younger."

"Who cares? Does that make you better than me?"

"No, not at all," he says, flustered. "You were just so small that I thought—" I hold up my hand to cut him off. I don't want to hear his excuses about why he isn't *into me.*

"Really?" I snort. "That's your excuse? That I'm small? I'm five foot four."

Now he's giving me attitude. "That's not what I meant."

"Oh?" I tilt my head to the side. "Then tell me, Luke, what did you mean?"

He stutters, still holding my finger, but doesn't give me an answer. This time it's my turn to arch a brow.

"You know what, don't worry about it. You know why?"

I lean in close so that our lips almost touch, ignoring the crackle I feel between us. Slowly, I stand on the tips of my toes, and lifting my lashes to meet his gaze, I whisper, "You're not my type." I swear I caught him blushing before I turned around and walked right out of the break room.

Chapter Seven

I try to keep my breathing even as I greet my students with a smile. Thank God I kept my cool in front of Luke, because whatever that was in there now has me trembling.

"Guy problems?" Ally asks, her puppy dog eyes twinkling.

I place my hands on my hips and nearly whisper, "What makes you say that?"

"I can tell by the look on your face. It's the same look my mom has when she and my dad are arguing."

"I see." I pat her on the head and say, "Don't tell anyone, okay?"

"No worries. Your secret's safe with me."

"And don't you worry about me either. I'll be just fine." I wink.

She tilts her head, examining my face for deception. "Okay."

I point my finger at her. "I'm serious."

"I said okay." She smiles, and I smile back.

I've never been good at hiding my emotions. It's another trait I inherited from my father. "Today we'll continue to work on the power of the elbow," I say to my students. They all sit and listen contently. "Taylor, Maddy, come here. I want to do a demonstration and use you two as my examples." I look at Ally. "I'm a little terrified to use Ally again; anyway, I'm convinced she already has this down." I roll my eyes, and the girls laugh around me.

"Taylor, you're going to be the bad guy and grab Maddy from behind." I stand behind Maddy and wrap my arms around her, showing Taylor what she needs to do. "Maddy, I need you to pretend like you have no clue you're about to be attacked. Act oblivious." The girls giggle as they slip on the armor and get into their positions. I look to Taylor and Maddy. "While I am speaking to the class, I want you to demonstrate the moves as I say them. Got it?"

"Got it," the girls say back.

"Great." I lower my voice as if I'm telling a story. "Imagine you are caught off guard, and someone grabs you from behind. What do you do?"

"You scream 'No!'" Ally answers.

"That's right," I say. "Then what?"

"You use your elbows, knees, and head to hurt the attacker."

"That's good, Rylee. Other than hurting your attacker, what are you trying to accomplish?" I ask.

"To get far away from them!" shouts Ally.

"Good girl. Now let's say your attacker is behind you, and you feel like his or her face is close enough for you to hurt them. Where do you hurt them, and what do you use? Show us Maddy."

Maddy jabs Taylor right in the nose, and it's a good thing she's wearing a mask. "Good job, Maddy," I say, as the rest of the class claps. Taylor shakes her head as if the blow made her dizzy.

"You okay?"

"I'm good," she says.

"Where's another place you can hit the attacker, using your elbow?" I ask.

"The neck," Rylee answers. I nod and point to Taylor while she holds her hand up.

"The eyes."

"Uh huh, and what's another place, Ally?" I ask, pointing to her.

"The ears."

"That's right. Good job girls." I clap. "You're all doing great! I'm so proud of you!" *I really am. They've come a long way.* We play along like this for a while, using several different positions until the class ends, and I head back to the locker room.

"Reese," Kyle calls me over.

"What's up?"

"Pam called, and I told her you were busy with your class."

I bite my lip. "Did she need anything?"

"She said she wanted to talk to you about arrangements she made with Luke—about you two working together."

"What do you mean *arrangements?*" I glance behind the desk to see what he's so consumed with. He's playing some silly game on his phone.

"She didn't say," he says, shrugging his shoulders. "She just told me to have you ask Luke." He punches a few buttons, and I stare in disbelief.

"Are you kidding me?"

He shakes his head. "Nope." I want to throw his phone into the trashcan. Instead I just grab it, finally getting his full attention.

"Kyle, are you sure she didn't say anything else? Like what Luke and I are supposed to be working on?"

He narrows his eyes and reaches for his phone. "I'm sure. She said she might not have time to call back and to have you ask Luke."

"Right. Because they're so tight now," I growl, not waiting for him to answer back.

I make my way over to the weight machines to blow off steam. Glancing in the mirror, I see Luke working on the heavy bag. He's swinging right, left, right, left, in slow controlled movements. He's focused, like a natural, ready and determined to fulfill his task. I can understand why he's won so many titles. There's something dangerous about the look in his eyes. He's like a predator circling his prey, planning the precise moment of attack. As I stand there and watch him, I'm put in a trance, calculating each and every move, as he captivates me. I can't tear my eyes away, and before I know it, I'm stepping closer—until I lose my train of thought when he catches me.

In a flash, I remove my eyes from his body, praying he didn't notice me ogling him. *What in the world was I thinking?* I clench my fists at my sides as I speed walk toward the locker room.

"Reese, hold up!" Luke shouts. I walk faster. I don't want to see his face, especially after our talk. So I pretend I don't hear him, keeping my head trained to the floor. With that, he leaves me alone, and I'm thankful.

"I'm leaving, Kyle," I say over my shoulder, before I step into the locker room to grab my stuff.

"Later."

It's late, and eerily quiet out here. I'm regretting not bringing my car. What Gia said is right. I need to think about my safety. But my apartment is less than a mile away, and it's not like I haven't done this before. The past couple weeks have been crazy, and I've been eating nothing but a bunch of crap; I figure it won't hurt to exercise.

The night air is warm, but I welcome the small breeze striding forward. There's about a month or two left of this hot Phoenix weather, and I can't wait for the change in late fall.

I hear the faint patter of footsteps following behind me. With the Packers guy's words fresh in my mind, I picture the creepy look in his eyes as his fingers touched my skin, and how his friends enjoyed the way he made me squirm. The sound becomes louder, alerting me to pick up my pace. Whoever's behind me is gaining ground, as if they're coming after me. Well let them come, because I'm ready and trained to kick some serious ass!

I turn around and shout, "No," just as I aim my knee at his groin. He jumps out of the way, blocking me with his hands. So I go for the eyes, but that doesn't work either. When he just stands there, as if I'm not a challenge, not even trying to restrain me, my temper explodes. I swing wildly, using everything I know to take him down. There's only one of them. This shouldn't be so difficult. I use my fists, elbows, and knees, yet nothing seems to faze him. Then he wraps his arms around me, and holds me still, attempting to calm me with his words.

"Shh," he says softly. "I'm not going to hurt you."

I'm shaking, gripping his shirt, with no idea what came over me. I just attacked an innocent man, right outside of the parking lot, for no apparent reason at all. I lift my lashes, and he slowly loosens his grip. The way he's watching me with genuine concern feels comforting, familiar, safe.

"I … I'm sorry, Luke," my voice cracks as I try to make sense of why I attacked him. He isn't the creep pervert with the jacked up, yellow teeth. He's the person who seems fixed on protecting me. "I don't know what came over me."

He scans my face. "You don't need to explain. I get it."

"You do?" I ask. "Cuz I don't."

He runs a hand through his hair, taking a couple steps backward. He looks stressed.

"Why are you out here?"

"To give you a ride." His voice is soft. "Now that you know you're not as tough as you think, will you let me?" There's that cocky smile I love to hate. "Give you a ride I mean?" He's right. He dodged everything I threw at him, and I feel stupid.

Resigning, I walk right past him and throw my arms in the air. "Fine. You win. Take me home."

He snorts. "Thanks for the favor."

"Anytime. By the way, do you have a car?"

"I've got a truck at home. Why?"

"Because I don't do motorcycles, and I'm not thrilled about riding on yours."

He looks me up and down, which isn't a pretty picture. I'm wearing a pair of sweats and a ratty old t-shirt. The corner of his mouth tips. "There's a first time for everything princess." He hands me a helmet and helps me place it on my head, securing hit. Then gets on the Harley first and signals for me to get on next.

"Does your girlfriend ride on your bike?" I bat my eyelashes when he turns around to answer me.

"Is that your way of asking if I have a girlfriend?" *Cocky son of a bitch!*

Giving him a fake smile, I reply, "Only in your dreams, lover boy."

He flashes his dimples. "Now I know I'm not your type, but you're gonna have to wrap your arms around me real tightly, all right?"

I roll my eyes.

"I wouldn't want you falling off." He winks.

"Real funny," I say, wrapping my arms around his waist.

He starts up the bike then says, "A little tighter."

Chapter Eight

Reese

Sweat slowly trickles down the top of my lip, leaving a nasty salty taste on my tongue. I hear the sound of a door open and shut then watch him walk to the end of the driveway. He carries soap, a bucket, and a handful of towels, before placing them in a pile on the ground. "Hi," I yell out.

He responds with a kind smile. "What's your name?" His eyes are squinting from the brightness of the sun.

"Reese." I smile back, looking over at the new car parked in his driveway. "Do you drive?"

He nods his head. "Well, I've got my permit."

"Is that your car?" I ask, pointing at it.

"It will be." His arms stretch back and pull off his shirt, showing off the hard lines of his arms, chest, and stomach. My eyes go wide for reasons I don't quite understand. All of the sudden, my body feels funny, and I can't seem to find my voice. I turn around and finish my chores without saying another word. Thinking to myself that he probably doesn't want to talk to a ten-year-old girl anyway.

When my father comes home he calls me outside. It's not hard to notice he's been drinking. "I told you to have your chores done by the time I got home!"

I stand speechless, confused as to why he's shouting. "I did them. I'm done," I stutter, looking around the yard to see what I missed.

"Really?" he asks, raising his eyebrows. I hesitantly nod my head yes. "You lying to me, girl?" His hand lifts to strike me, and I close my eyes waiting for the blow.

"Probably not a good idea to hit your little girl, Mr. Johnson," the boy interrupts. I open my eyes and stare at my father as his head whips around to face him.

"Mind your own business, if you know what's good for you, boy. I know who you are," my father tells him. His voice is hard and scary. I hold my breath, terrified that my father might hurt him.

"It would be a shame if the public found out you've been beating your wife and daughter." My mouth drops wide open in disbelief. I've never heard anyone talk to my father this way—let alone a kid—but I like it; I envy him for his courage. My father says nothing in response, but you can tell he's bothered. Instead, he grabs me by the arm, and pulls me over to a bag of leaves, suddenly reminding me that I forgot to throw it in the garbage can. Pointing to it he asks, "What's this?"

"I'm s-sorry. I just forgot," I say, my voice shaking.

"Don't let it happen again," he growls then turns around and walks inside. I sigh in relief and look back to silently thank the boy, but to my disappointment, he's gone. Suddenly, I realize that I never even got his name.

I get up early so I can have more time before my class begins. I want to get a work out in and hit the heavy bag. I'm taken by surprise when I enter the parking lot and see Luke stepping out of a black, older model Chevy truck. He's wearing gray track pants and a white t-shirt that fits his broad shoulders and chest perfectly. Those seem to be common color choices for him. "Hey." I smile. "Is that your truck?"

He smiles back. "It is. You sound surprised." We meet in the middle and walk side by side toward the entrance.

"I just expected you to drive something new, with all the bells and whistles."

"Oh yeah, why'd you expect that?"

Shrugging my shoulders, I reply, "I don't know. You just seem like the kind of guy that would want to have it all." I'm not really sure why I'm making this assumption.

"What kind of guy is that?" He stops, cocking a brow.

"I don't know, the professional fighter kind, I guess."

He tilts his head. "Do you know a lot of professional fighters?" His eyes sparkle in amusement.

I open my mouth then shut it, because I don't. "Okay, you got me. I don't know any personally. I guess I just assumed."

"You do that a lot."

After an hour of cardio, I make my way over to the heavy bag, put on the boxing gloves, and start swinging. This time I try to keep my composure, knowing I could have an audience.

Luke comes over and stands with his arms crossed, leaning against the wall as he watches me. His eyes are intense, as they always seem to be, and I can't help but find him a little distracting. "Make sure you swing like this," he says, showing me the proper movement. I watch him, intrigued as he displays the right way to move my body. "I don't want you to get yourself injured." His eyes are sincere.

Although I'm embarrassed that I need his help, I swallow my pride and take his advice. "Wow, I can already tell the difference."

"See what I mean?"

"I do. Thanks!" I smile, but he's pursing his lips as if he's having a hard time *not* saying something. "Spit it out, Luke."

He laughs once then runs a hand through his hair. "Have you talked to Pam?"

I stop. "No. She called, but I missed it." Then I remember what Kyle said about Luke and me working together.

In a hushed tone, he says, "I don't start teaching for another two weeks. Until then, Pam asked me to team up with you."

I looked into his eyes. "Okayyy. Is that it?" Because the way he's acting right now makes me think there's more.

The corner of his mouth tips. "She also asked if I would teach you some jiu-jitsu. So you can implement what you learn into your class. She said some of the parents have been requesting it, and she was hoping we would try it out."

Again, I can't help but notice how amazing he smells, and the way it's affecting my senses. I feel that strange familiarity as he watches my face, waiting for my response. So I just stand there nodding my head as I process what he told me. "It's weird. There's something about you that feels so familiar, and this isn't the first time I've felt it. It's almost like déjà vu."

He runs a hand over his face, glancing around the room before his eyes land on me. "That is weird." Then moving along, he asks, "So, you're okay with that?"

"Huh? Oh the training? Are you kidding? I would love it!"

He looks surprised by my answer and raises his brows. "Where is Reese, and what have you done with her?"

I playfully swat his arm. "What do you mean?"

"What do you mean, what do I mean? You hate me," he says, pointing a finger at his own chest.

Throwing my gloved hands against my hips, I frown. "I don't … I don't hate you." I never said that out loud, did I? Truthfully, I don't.

He snorts. "Could have fooled me."

"Well, I'm sorry if I gave you that impression," I say sincerely, because I do actually feel bad for the way that I've treated him.

He chuckles. "Well you have been pretty vocal about the kind of person you think I am, and last night you tried to kick my ass, so ..."

"Ugh," I shut my eyes. "You're right. I misjudged you, so can we start over?"

His eyes sparkle, and he reaches out to shake my hand and grins. "Friends?" He helps me pull the glove off my hand.

"Friends," I answer, pausing before I ask, "So when are we supposed to do this?"

"Pam suggested after-hours or before we open. We'll just work it around our schedules." He walks over to the row of chairs and takes a seat, so I take the one next to him.

"Are they paying you?"

"No," he says quietly then clears his throat.

"They should," I frown.

"Pam offered, but I declined." He shrugs.

My mouth drops, completely surprised. "Why would you do that?"

"What?" He smirks sitting back in the chair. "I don't mind training you. I'd like to help." This guy is not at all like I thought.

I tilt my head, trying to figure him out. "Really?"

"Really," he says sincerely.

"How do you know Pam anyway?" I ask.

Running a hand through his messy hair, he sighs. "We go way back."

I look down at my hands and mumble, "Yeah so do we." I smile. "We used to be neighbors actually." I lift my lashes, finding his eyes are resting on my scar, the one that's slightly hidden above my brow. Then something in his gaze causes a rash of chills to spread over my entire body, and my heart pounds rapidly, as the realization suddenly hits me. I know him.

Chapter Nine

Reese

"When I was ten I fell off my bike." I hesitate. "My face landed in the rocks, and I got this ugly scar." It's a lie, but I watch for his reaction.

Slowly, he reaches over and gently brushes his thumb across my scar, as if he's washing it away. He gives the saddest smile I've ever seen. I have to squeeze my eyes shut to keep from crying. How could I have gone this long without recognizing him? The person I dream about nearly every night and never even knew his name. Luke, his name is Luke, and he saved me all those years ago. He saved me from Ronald and the abuse of my father. He saved my mother's life, and not once asked for anything in return. I'm a horrible person, the biggest bitch that ever walked the planet.

"You okay?" he asks, immediately snapping me awake. His eyes are soft, his lips pressed into a tight line. He knows who I am, and he's wondering if I've figured him out.

I stand up, brushing my palms over my pants. "Yeah I'm fine." I tuck a strand of hair behind my ear, and have a hard time looking him in the eyes. "I'm gonna take a bathroom break, then I'll catch you in class in about thirty minutes? I arch an eyebrow.

He watches me carefully, and I wonder if he can tell I'm lying. "Yeah," he hesitates, "see you over there." Then he looks in the other direction before I walk away from him.

"Just breathe, Reese." Gripping the edge of the counter, I stand in front of the mirror and talk to myself like a crazy person, repeatedly inhaling through my mouth and breathing out my nose. "Why wouldn't he tell me? Why wouldn't Pam tell me?" I think about the short time he lived there, how he left after my father's arrest, only to come back three years later, then leave again. "They never talked about him front of me, but then again, would I have noticed since I never knew his name?"

I throw my hair up in a high pony, wishing I would've fixed myself up a little this morning. "No wonder why he looked surprised when I told him my age," I grumble. "He still thinks of me as the little girl he always tried to protect. He's got to be what, about five or six years older than me? That's not that big of an age difference." I tuck away a straggling hair. "They must have some reason for not telling me." I frown. "Well, two can play at that game. I'll just act like I haven't figured it out—see how long it takes them to say something." A couple of ladies walk into the bathroom that I recognize as regulars. So I immediately stop talking to my reflection and tell them, "Hello."

They smile back, and one of them waves.

I spend the rest of my free time calming my nerves, as well as the crazy new feelings that are stirring. If I thought Luke affected me before, that has nothing on what he's doing to me now. "Class, this is Luke." I stand in the center of the octagon, and he's positioned right beside me. "He's going to be helping us for the next couple of weeks." Funny how when I say those words now, I feel my cheeks heat and my pulse speed up a bit.

He gives his heart-stopping grin that, most likely, many girls have dropped their panties for. "Hey ladies." He raises his hand in a small wave.

"Hey Luke," they all say at once, some of them giggling. Ally raises her arm, so I point to her.

"Ally."

"Is he your boyfriend?"

Luke and I chuckle, but her question makes me nervous. I clear my throat. "No, Ally, he just works here with me."

"Oh," she says back, then wiggles her index finger in a motion for me to come closer. I place my ear next to her mouth, and she whispers, "Is he the reason for the guy problems?" I turn and look into those puppy dog eyes and notice she's smiling, and I grin back. "He's really cute," she adds, flicking her gaze to Luke then back. I look over my shoulder as he asks each of the girls for their names, oblivious to our conversation.

Luke talks to the class about everything they're going to learn today. I sit back and watch as he gains twelve new fans. "How many of you ladies know what wrestling is?" he asks them.

All of them raise their hands, listening intently as he strides back and forth. I can already tell—based on how they watch him— he has a special way with them. Of course, the fact that he's gorgeous might have something to do with their immediate interest. "Reese and I are going to show you a form of martial arts called jiu-jitsu. Many people compare it to wrestling." I glance at the girls and spot a couple of them whispering, eyeing him as if he were a god. When they catch me watching them, I wink.

"With jiu-jitsu you take the fight to the mat. The fighter on the bottom has just as much advantage as the fighter on top. You just need to learn which strategy will work best, and that all depends on the position you're in, as well as your opponent. You understand?" He gives them a dimpled smile. They nod their heads, and he turns to me and mumbles, "Throw me to the ground. I'll go easy on you."

I wasn't sure I heard him right. "Huh?" I raise a brow, and he smirks. Okay, so I did hear him correctly. I dive head first into his stomach, wrapping my arms around his waist, and he falls easily— purposely.

"Stay on top of me," he murmurs.

Not a problem, I don't say out loud, feeling the ridges of his body underneath me. I can tell he's speaking to the girls, but haven't heard a single thing he's saying, because my hormones have now decided to go into hyper-drive. I mean, how can someone smell so incredibly intoxicating? I could really get used to this. In fact, I don't want to let him up.

The sound of twelve giggling girls snaps me out of my daze. Then I feel Luke's rumbling laughter penetrate through my chest and trickle into my hair. *Oh my God! Was I really just sniffing him?* My cheeks heat, and I lift my lids, meeting his wide grin. "Sorry about that," I say, mortified I did that in front of the entire class.

His eyes twinkle. "Don't worry about it. Do I stink?" He brushes his hand up my back before he lifts his arm to smell himself. I can't help but tremble a little at the intimate touch.

"Uh no," I answer, chewing on my lip then add, "You smell great actually." The corner of his mouth curls, and I glance at the students with their gaze pinned in our direction, as if waiting for something to happen. I clear my throat. "Moving along to the next part of today's lesson," Luke continues as if nothing ever happened.

"Okay ladies, as Reese lays across my body, I'm going to secure my left leg high up on her thigh area like this." He scoots my body up so that our faces are almost level, while his foot securely hooks underneath my thigh.

I can feel every hard line and ripple that belongs to him. It's beginning to be a problem since I'm having a terrible time controlling my hormones. I'm not very experienced when it comes to the opposite sex, and it just so happens that this particular male underneath me is the only one who seems to affect me. I squeeze my eyes shut, mentally counting to ten.

"You okay?" he asks. His caramel-colored orbs scan my face, with no humor in them.

"Yeah, I'm fine," I say weakly, embarrassed by my body's reaction to his closeness.

He watches me a little longer to make sure.

"Really, I'm okay." I give a small smile.

The corner of his mouth tips. "Okay." He turns and faces the class. "When I'm confident it's secure, I'm going to rotate my hips and slide out from underneath her. I want you all to watch me, so pay attention."

My pulse quickens. What? Rotate his hips? Good Lord. Then, before I can blink, Luke flips me over, pinning me down, so he's on top of me.

"Wow," I hear some of the girls say.

Yeah... wow. I pant underneath him. I don't know if I'm supposed to move or just lay here and enjoy this. Right now I'll take the latter. I gaze into his handsome face as he continues to explain how he got me here. Right now, I don't even care. I'm not listening to a single word that leaves his mouth. I'm just trying to get my breathing back to normal and my heart rate to slow down.

"Do you girls want to try it?" he asks. Not once has he looked at me since we flipped. Because this doesn't affect him! Because he thinks I'm just a *kid*! "It's called a jailbreak." He smiles.

The girls happily say, "Yes." He stands up and holds out his hand, relieving me from the weight of his body. His eyes linger, and I take it, before he looks away. The girls team up and practice the rest of the class period, and everything runs smoothly.

"Thank you," I say after the kids leave, but I'm thankful for much more than I let on.

Eyeing me curiously, his mouth stretches in a wry grin. "I'm sorry I took over your class." He runs a hand through his hair and adds, "I kind of have a thing with control."

You don't say? "It's fine. I mean... don't worry about it. I didn't mind."

He cocks a brow and takes a step closer. "What was that?" His tone is playful. He dips his face lower to look into my eyes.

"You heard me." I bite back a smile, feeling myself blush.

"No. I don't think I did." He lifts my chin with his finger and says, "Could you repeat that, please?" Then he smiles. He's so close, his minty breath falls against my face.

"Wh...what would you like me to repeat?" I stutter softly, feeling like my insides are on fire.

His eyes sparkle. "You said you love it when I take control of your class."

My mouth drops open, and I glare. "I did not!"

He roars in laughter, and I swat him. "Ow!" He flinches.

"Take it back, Ryann!" I swing at him again.

"Okay, okay, I take it back." He holds up his hands. "You like to have the control." He flashes his dimples, and it's the happiest I've ever seen him.

"That's better," I say, pointing, tucking a loose strand of hair behind my ear. "But in all seriousness… the class went well." I shrug.

"The girls enjoyed working with you." We start walking toward the entrance to get our stuff.

"You think?" He looks surprised that I would say such a thing.

"Yeah, I think." Reaching behind the desk to grab my purse, I turn to him and add, "You're good with them."

"Thanks." The corner of his mouth curls. "I think that's the nicest thing I've ever heard you say to me."

I frown and start walking to the door, but he stops me when he reaches out and gently touches my hair. "You missed one," His voice is soft—sweet.

"Oh." My pulse races again. "Thanks." My goodness, what the hell is wrong with me? I feel an involuntary shiver and silently pray he doesn't notice.

He clears his throat.

Oh God, he probably did notice.

"Did I hurt you earlier?" We push through the exit, and he watches me intently.

I tilt my head, confused. "No, when?"

"Earlier, on the mat." He licks his lips, and my eyes follow. "I could feel your heartbeat. It was going pretty fast."

My cheeks must have been blood red. *How in the world am I going to be able to train with this man? PRIVATELY?* "No, you didn't hurt me." My eyes drop to the ground. "Not at all."

"Good." He runs a hand over the back of his neck. "Oh, and just so you know, when we train together..." He smirks, then leaning in, he whispers against my ear, "I'm the one in control."

I blink a couple times, opening my mouth to argue, but decide against it.

Pulling away, he gazes into my eyes. "Can you handle that?" He's still whispering.

I feel my cheeks heat. I want to say, *Actually, I don't know if I can.* Instead I answer, "Yeah, I think I can handle it," in a funny voice that I don't recognize. *The cocky son of a bitch can probably do anything he wants talking to me like that!*

His mouth turns up. "Good."

Chapter Ten

Reese

"You ready?" Gia asks. I hear her bracelets clinking together as she waltzes into my room." I give her a once-over appreciating her striking blue maxi dress, which accentuates her eyes, but then frown at my own outfit, because it pales in comparison.

"Almost," I tell her reflection. I lean over the counter to finish putting on my lip-gloss. "By the way, that dress really makes your eyes pop."

"Why thank you!" She smiles, batting her eyelashes.

"You always look good though." I point to her dress. "I need something like that."

"You need everything." She gazes into the mirror, making a fish face as she fiddles with pieces of her hair. "It's your own fault. I've been trying to get you to go for a while."

"I haven't been able to afford it," I scoff. "Otherwise I would have." I walk over to my closet and slip on my shoes as she dismisses my response. Gia always tells me not to give my mother money, and it usually turns into an argument. "You ready to go?"

"Yeah." She takes a step back and arches a brow. "What's up with the lights?"

I roll my eyes. "I know … they flicker like this place is haunted. You get what you pay for I guess."

"Ugh. That would drive me crazy." She turns around and walks out my bedroom door then looks over her shoulder. "How about I drive, and you finish telling me about Luke?"

I grab my purse off the bed and dig for my keys. "Okay, sounds good." We lock up my apartment and make our way out to Gia's brand new BMW. It's a five series, white, and it's my dream car. "I'm so jealous."

"You want to drive her?" She reaches out to give me the keys.

I would love to, but I'm scared I'll ruin her somehow. "Not yet." I open the passenger door and get in. "She's too pretty, I'm afraid I'll scratch her."

"Your loss," she answers as we buckle ourselves in. "Now tell me about what happened, and I want details." I flinch before she turns down the blaring stereo after starting the ignition.

"You were jamming, weren't you?"

She grips the steering wheel. "I always turn it up when I'm by myself. Okay, back to Luke."

I fidget a little at the thought of him. "Remember how Luke has connections with Jim and Pam, and I wasn't really sure how?" I glance at her, waiting.

"Uh huh," she answers, her eyes focused on the road as she pulls out of the complex.

"Then I told you how Luke is real protective of me, calling me *kid* on several different occasions, and how I overheard the conversation he had with Kyle. I arch a brow until she replies, making sure she's paying attention.

"Yesss," she drags out the word then quickly glances at me. "Get on with it."

"You are not going to believe this," I say seriously, because I know she's going to flip. Closing my eyes I take a deep breath then say it. "It's him, Gia."

She tilts her head to the side. "Who?"

"Luke is, *him*," I reply sternly, holding my hands out, as if he's standing right in front of the car, but it still doesn't register. "The boy from my past, the one I dream about, the one that used to live across the street."

She slams on the brakes, and I immediately grab the dashboard for support. "Shit! I'm sorry," she shouts, quickly pulling over to the side of the road. Her eyes narrow, "No way."

I nod my head. "Yes way."

"How do you know? I mean like, how did you find out?"

"We haven't talked about it, but it finally clicked when I caught him looking at my scar."

She looks at me, confused. "So, you think he knows who you are?"

"I do."

"But why wouldn't he say anything?"

"I have no idea, but I'm not saying a word until he does. Two can play that game."

We both laugh. Then Gia says, "You're bad."

"I'm careful. There's got to be a reason he hasn't said anything."

"Do you think it's a sign?" Her eyes twinkle, and she reaches for my hand excitedly.

"What do you mean a 'sign'?"

Leaning in closer, she says, "I mean, he's in our class, you're working together, then he shows up at Chili's and gives you a ride home." She shakes her head. "Maybe everything is happening the way it's supposed to happen."

I ponder that for a second—how he came to my rescue when my father was drunk and out of control, and another time I'd rather not think about. Today's supposed to be a good day. I don't want to mess it up with thoughts of my past. "It's probably a strange coincidence." Shrugging my shoulders, I add, "I don't really believe in fate."

"It explains why you are the way you are."

I look at her, confused.

"You know … with guys."

"You mean … not interested? Judgmental? Unavailable?" I mumble, moving my gaze to the windshield.

"What if he's like… your soulmate?" she murmurs, ignoring my question.

I flick my eyes in her direction, and the grin she's holding stretches so wide I wonder if it hurts.

"Soulmate?"

"Yeah, soulmate."

"We can barely even stand each other." I chew on my nails, feeling vulnerable. "He doesn't look at me that way."

She snorts. "Sure he doesn't, and stop biting your nails. That's gross." She pulls my hand away from my mouth, and I give her a glare. "Are you interested in him? I mean, now that you know who he is?"

"I don't know what I'm feeling," I growl.

"So you *do feel* something for him then?"

I blow out a nervous breath. "I care about him," I say softly. "I always have. There's sort of this connection with him."

She grins, moving her eyebrows up and down. "And you're attracted to him, right? You'd be blind not to be." I picture the way his eyes pierce into mine, and how I feel when he touches me—his sexy hair, his tattoos, all of him.

"I'm crazy attracted to him," I answer, biting on my lip. "I hate it."

She laughs. "Why do you hate it?"

I cover my face with my hands, peeking through my fingers. "Because I'm used to being pursued and uninterested. Being the pursuer is new to me. I've never had to fight my attraction to someone. God Gia, when he's close to me it's almost unbearable."

"So don't fight it." She frowns. "Problem solved."

I wish it were that easy.

"I'm not the kind of girl to make the first move." I sigh. "I wouldn't even know how, and I don't deal well with rejection. Honestly, I'd rather be alone."

Her eyes narrow. "He cares about you. He's not your father, Reese. You're reading him wrong."

"I didn't say he was." Looking down at my hands, I continue, "I know he cares, but it's in the way a big brother cares for his kid sister."

"You told him you're twenty, right?"

"Yeah."

"And how did he react?"

I think back to the look on his face when I told him my age. "He looked surprised, actually."

"Good," she says, biting back a grin, and I can see the wheels spinning in her eyes, before she looks for other vehicles and steers back onto the road.

"Seriously, Gia. I'm not going to throw myself at him. That's not me."

She shakes her head. "Of course not! We'll make him come to you." The look on her face says she's up to no good, but I smile anyway.

"I'm afraid to ask what's going on in that brain of yours."

"Don't be." She giggles deviously. "Soon and very soon, you're going to have Luke Ryann eating out of the palm of your hand."

I arch a brow. "Oh really? And what sort of magic tricks are we pulling out of our asses for that to happen?"

Pursing her lips, she eyes me from head to toe. "First, we'll start with a new wardrobe. We can work on the rest later. That is— if we need to."

I open my mouth to respond then realize I haven't told her about the private lessons. "Oh my gosh! I completely forgot!" I grab her arm. "Pam asked Luke to train me after hours. He's going to be teaching me jiu-jitsu for my class."

"SHUT ... UP." Her mouth falls wide open.

"It's the truth." I give her my serious face. "We'll be spending practically every day together." As soon as the words leave my lips, tiny bumps appear all over my skin, sending a slight shiver all over. Gia twists the dial to the AC, and I decide not to bother telling her the real reason behind my trembling.

She narrows her eyes. "What do you mean 'train you'?"

My hands fidget in my lap. "Exactly what I said," I pause. "I'll be the student, and Luke will be my teacher."

"You're kidding me, right?"

I shake my head no.

Gia points at me. "You're saying that you two are going to be wrestling around, hot and sweaty, limbs tangled up in each other, and you're going to be *alone*?"

"That's what I'm saying," I answer flatly, although the picture that just ran through my mind makes me blush. My head slams against the headrest when she stomps on the brakes again. "Ow!"

"This is going to be great!" she says, beaming, completely ignoring my outburst. "We'll get you some hot little workout outfits." She places her hand on my knee. "We'll make sure they're classy, not trashy. Do you still wear those frumpy sweats and oversized t-shirts?" She glances at me, raising her eyebrows.

"Yes." I frown.

Shaking her head back and forth, she replies, "Never again. You have an amazing figure. Time to show it off."

"You sound like my mother," I snort, but maybe she has a point. I've never been one that dresses to impress.

"You have no idea how excited I am," she says, pulling into the mall parking lot. We climb out of the car and make our way toward the entrance.

"I'm beginning to have an idea."

Chapter Eleven

Reese

I had already purchased several workout outfits, a handful of form-fitting tops, four dresses, and three pairs of stilettos. Gia's desperate to find a certain brand of workout shorts. She tells me they'll do wonders for my big, curvy butt. Okay, maybe she didn't use those words, but that's the way I heard them.

"This is cute." She holds up a piece of fabric resembling either a tube top or maybe even a skirt.

"I teach children Gia," I remind her.

She frowns and says, "Oh yeah, I forgot." Then her eyes light up. "You could always change before for class."

I picture myself muttering excuses for my wardrobe changes. "Don't you think that's a little too obvious?"

She examines the material she's holding. "Yeah, maybe you're right."

"His head is big enough as it is." I picture his cocky grin as he figures out I'm dressing for him. "I want him to notice me, without knowing that it was my intention." I point at the fabric. "How would I even wear that?"

She giggles, setting down the questionable item before we make our way over to the sale rack. "Here they are," she shouts then grabs a pair of black stretchy shorts that look like they're made of spandex.

I drop my gaze to my hips and thighs. "I don't know."

"Stop it!" She swats me. "They're going to look great. You'll see."

I feel the stretchy material. "They feel comfortable."

She nods her head in agreement. "They come in several different colors, too." Grabbing a couple pairs, she hands them to me. "Trust me, they're hot. Now hurry and try them on. I'm getting hungry," she says, as she shoos me towards the fitting room. I hurry along and do what she tells me.

"You look exactly how I pictured," Gia squeals. "Woman! You are rockin' those shorts!"

I place my hands on my hips then look over my shoulder, checking my reflection from the back. "Huh." I'm surprised that I like what I see. "They're not too bad, are they?" I mumble to myself, although Gia can hear me.

A smile crawls across her face. "They're perfect," she replies. She buys me a pair in every color and refuses to take my money.

As soon as I'm back at my apartment I decide to try Pam. I've been hoping I'd get a chance to talk to her before I see Luke again. There are a lot of things I want to say, and many questions I need to ask. So I punch in her number, surprised when she answers on the first ring.

"Reese?" I can tell she's excited. She may even be a little tipsy.

"Hey." I smile—glad she's happy. Jim had said that the last trip he dragged her on, she complained and had a miserable time. "Are you having fun?"

"I am," she giggles. "Can you tell?"

I laugh along with her, picturing her sitting by the pool with an apple martini, wearing one of those big hats. "Maybe just a little. Are you hanging around a more entertaining crowd or what?" I kick off my shoes and swing my legs over the arm of my couch.

"Definitely. Do you remember Kellie Nichole? She's been in the gym a few times. She's brunette, has shoulder-length hair, and always wears those funky black-rimmed glasses?"

I search my brain for someone with that description. "No, the name doesn't ring a bell."

"Hmm, well anyway, she's a riot. We've kept each other busy while the hubbies do their thing. We've been window-shopping, enjoying drinks by the pool, and we're scheduled to get facials in about an hour. It's definitely made my trip, having her with me. I usually stay cooped up in the hotel," she scoffs. "Jim couldn't pay me to go to one of those meetings."

A smile plays at my lips. "I don't know why you go at all."

"I *am* his wife. I've got to be somewhat supportive." She sighs.

"You're right, and you're a good wife, Pam." I grin.

"I know," she kids.

"Well, I'm glad you're having a good time." I bite at my nails, 'cause that's what I do when I'm nervous.

"Me too. By the way, how are the classes going? How's Luke doing with the girls?" *Here we go.*

I hesitate before answering. The mention of his name makes my heart speed up. "He's great actually. The girls love him."

"That's good," she replies softly. "And I'm sorry I didn't get a chance to tell you ahead of time. I just got so preoccupied with this trip that I forgot."

My hand starts hurting from the tight grip I have on the phone, so I switch ears to give it a rest. "I understand," I answer, waiting for her to continue, but she doesn't. Then I decide to throw her a bone. "So, how do you know Luke?"

"Well, I uh …" she stutters. "We uh … Jim and I …"

"He told you not to tell me. Didn't he?" I interrupt, not letting her finish.

She sighs into the phone. "I'm sorry, Reese. He was worried you would feel uncomfortable."

Uncomfortable? "Why?" I frown.

"I asked him the same thing. He said, the last time he saw you …"

"Was when I was nearly raped," I whisper softly before adding, "I'm not broken, you know."

"I know," she says soothingly. "He just wanted to be careful, that's all. He's been through a lot himself. He knows how traumatic experiences can affect a person.

"Huh," is all I respond, too busy thinking about her words. I get off the couch and strip off my clothes, making my way over to the hamper. "What happened to him, Pam? Why did they put him in foster care?"

"That is something you need to ask him."

I frown. "Is there anything you can tell me? Like how old he is exactly?"

She chuckles softly. "Let's see. Well, he's twenty-five," then wistfully she adds, "he's about six feet three inches tall, extremely handsome." Her voice gets higher when she asks, "Wouldn't you say he's handsome?"

"Yeah, he's handsome," I answer, using my best attempt to sound nonchalant. "He knows it, too." I couldn't help it. I just had to say it.

"He's a good man, Reese, and he's done pretty well for himself considering the childhood his father gave him. Jim and I tried everything we could to get him out of that environment, but the state refused to let us adopt. We bought the car and stayed in contact through a cell phone, and on rare occasions, he'd come visit us at church. It was how we were able to keep in touch. Sure, he's had some trouble, but we could never be prouder of him than we are right now."

"Wow," is all I say because I can't seem to form any other words. "Was his father like mine, then? Was he abusive?" I picture a smaller version of Luke getting shoved around.

"I'm not going to get into details, but I will say, that he was— still is—much worse than your father. You're going to have to ask Luke if you want anything else," she replies, sounding a little stressed. Then adds, "Sorry, I just can't."

I feel like a jerk for bothering her on vacation. "I'm sorry for bringing this up now. I should have waited." I sit on the floor of my closet and straighten out my shoes.

"Don't be ridiculous! I'm glad you called." I can tell her response is genuine. "You know every now and then," she pauses, "Luke would ask about you."

I stop what I'm doing, unable to keep a smile from sliding across my face. *He asked about me?* "He did?"

"Yep. Before he left, he made us promise to look out for you."

Those words make my heart melt. It's like he was born to be my protector. I think it's sort of cute. "So how did he get into fighting anyway?" I ask, even though it's none of my business.

"She sighs. "He found a place where he could release his aggression, and it didn't take long to learn he was a natural. Within a short period of time he built a name for himself, making a large amount of money through fights and advertisements. He was only eighteen when it all started for him. After that, everything happened so fast."

"That's impressive."

"It is, but what's even more impressive is what he chose to do with his money."

I can tell the alcohol's kicking in, so I stop her, before she gets into trouble. "Pam, are you going to be late for your facial?"

"Oh shoot! What time is it?" I hear her ask someone away from the phone.

"I gotta go," she says, frazzled.

"That's fine. Oh, and Pam?" I ask before she can hang up.

"Yes?"

"Can you please not tell Luke that I figured out who he is?" I squeeze my eyes shut, praying she'll keep this a secret.

It takes a while for her to answer, but she finally says, "I don't like lying to him Reese, but I'll give you a little time. You should tell him."

"I will. Promise," I say, after letting out a breath. "I just need to figure out how." I throw on a t-shirt and plop down on my bed, sinking into the mattress.

"You'll be fine. I better get going, though."

"Oh jeez." I glance at the clock. "I'm sorry. If I don't hear from you, I'll see you when you get back."

"Okay, and I don't think we'll be back in time for the annual party," she whines. "But if you have any problems, call us."

"Oh, okay I will."

I hang up the phone and quickly drift off to sleep, preparing for my private lesson with Luke.

Chapter Twelve

It's Saturday morning. The first day Luke and I work on submission techniques. This means we'll spend plenty of time on the mats. Following Gia's advice, I put on a form-fitting purple tank, and pair it with black, booty-flattering shorts. I've probably checked my reflection fifty times, but finally force myself to walk out the door.

As I make my way into the gym, the first thing I notice is the place is dead quiet. It's just another reminder that Luke and I will be in here alone. When I round the corner I see him. His back is to me, and it looks like he's flipping through CDs—probably looking for music to drown out the uncomfortable silence. He's wearing his usual track pants and what looks to be an Under Armour shirt that fits his broad shoulders perfectly. Once I realize I'm about to drool, I forcefully tear my eyes away. "Hey," I finally say.

He glances over his shoulder. "Hey." As soon as his eyes land on my body, they widen, slowly drifting down every part, and linger on their way back up. Not knowing what to do with my hands, I fidget nervously from the heat of his gaze. He blinks a couple times then turns back around, saying nothing.

"Everything okay?" I ask, trying my best to sound unaffected.

It takes a while for him to answer when he finally says, "Yeah, why?" He keeps his head down as he picks through the rest of the CDs. I try to think of a good response, then he holds up a finger and reaches into his pocket. "Hold that thought," he says, pressing his phone to his ear. "Hey Lo, what's up?" And he walks right out of the room.

My heart sinks. *Lo? As in his girlfriend, Lauren?* The euphoria I was feeling a second ago quickly fades. I turn away, trying to get myself together before he comes back. I don't want to think about the beautiful blonde I'm competing with. It feels better to pretend she doesn't exist.

I twiddle my thumbs and mess with my hair, impatiently waiting for him to finish. I'm startled when I hear him say, "It's fine. You had no choice."

I turn at the waist, spotting him standing close behind me, his left hand resting firmly on his hip. "Don't put up with any more of his shit, Lauren," he says, before his eyes meet mine. "Love you too," he finishes.

I feel sick. I pray it doesn't show on my face.

"Later." He sets his phone on the floor next to my bag, and I try my best to appear naturally unbothered—like my heart wasn't just crushed into a million little pieces.

I lift my eyes and ask, "Some guy bothering your girlfriend?"

Scratching his head, he furrows his brows. "My what?"

"Your girlfriend ... Lauren." I lick my lips that have instantly gone dry then sit on the ground. "Is she okay?"

He watches me curiously, before his eyes turn playful, catching me by surprise. "Lauren's fine." He sits facing me then reaches out and tucks a loose strand of hair behind my ear.

Tiny bumps appear on my skin, and I feel myself blush. "Do you want to talk about it?" I ask, hoping to distract him.

He shrugs. "There's really nothing to say." Glancing at my arms, he adds, "Are you cold?" Very gently he runs his finger down my shoulder, and I do everything in my power not to a shiver.

Seriously? Can I hide nothing from this man? In the most convincing voice I can muster I reply, "It's a little chilly, but I can handle it."

The corner of his mouth tips. "Can you?" He stands up, making his way over to the stereo, and my eyes follow. Then he gracefully strides back in my direction. The man is sexy—too sexy for his own good ... or mine. "You ready?" he asks.

More than ever, I want to tell him, but instead I just say, "Ready."

"All right, lay down. I want to show you something."

Is it just me, or did his voice sound funny when he said that? I do as I'm told, feeling my cheeks heat after he sits down beside me.

My eyes lift to his face, finding a heart-stopping grin framed with two perfect dimples. "Did you go shopping?" he asks.

My breathing changes. "How'd you know?" I smile nervously, hoping he doesn't think he's the reason for it. I watch his teeth run across his bottom lip as his fingertips graze my thigh.

Tugging the edge of my shorts, he says, "You usually wear something ... a little less tight." Okay, so when he touched me, I stopped breathing. And then he has to go and say that!

"Excuse me ... less tight?" I scoot away from him, fuming. "You really are great with words, you know that?" I eye him up and down. "You should talk, show off! Your shirt looks like you bought it in the children's section. *Not really, but I'm pissed.*

He glances down at his shirt then rolls his eyes. "Will you calm down? I didn't mean it in a bad way. Every time I see you ..." He spreads his arms out. "You're clothes are like five sizes too big," he says, chuckling. "They never *fit* you *fit* you ... like that." His hand gestures to my clothes.

"What does that even mean?" I look at him like he's stupid. "And why didn't you just say that in the first place?"

He groans and runs a palm over his face. "Look, you're making this a way bigger deal than it is. Can we move on if I tell you the truth?"

I'm a little nervous about what the truth is, but I shrug and say, "Go for it," in a snotty tone that I can't help.

He purses his lips and his eyes drop all the way down to my toes before returning to my face. "I'm not sure if *I'll* be *comfortable* wrestling with you in that. Do you get what I'm saying?" His brows lift after speaking the words like he's talking to a toddler.

Huh?

When I tilt my head confused, he softly chuckles, adding, "I'm trying to be a gentleman here." The corner of his mouth tips. "Because I respect you."

Oh ... so he means? Mother of God, did he really just say that? Well hell, that was unexpected. I feel the blood rush straight to my cheeks, and my voice comes out in a squeak when all I'm able to say is, "Thank you."

"Sorry," Luke mumbles, sliding out from underneath me. He's been distracted and distant for the last hour, and it's really starting to get on my nerves.

"You're acting weird," I tell him, as he paces around the room for the tenth time. He stills and throws his hands on his hips, watching me carefully.

"What? Why are you looking at me like that?"

"Like what?" He cocks a brow.

"Like I have two heads?"

He drops his gaze to the floor and laughs lightly. "Lets try it again," he finally says, completely ignoring my question. "This time I'll go for your knees and ankles." Making his way back over, he adds, "Don't worry, I'll go easy on you. When we're done, you can try the same on me. Okay?" He arches a brow confidently. It makes me want to punch him, and lick him, all at the same time.

When I stop gawking, his words sink in, and I roll my eyes. "You think I'm weak."

He groans, clearly annoyed. "When did I give you that impression, Reese?"

My mouth drops. "Are you joking? Don't worry. I'll go easy on you," I mock.

He kneels down, forcing me to look at him. "Trust me. I don't think you're weak," his voice is kind, surprising me. "After a couple rounds, I'm going to make you work for it. Okay?" He grabs my hand to help me up, and my pulse races.

"Okay," I finally reply, once I'm confident I have a voice.

Without warning, he uses his foot, sweeping at my ankles. When I start to fall, he wraps his arms around the back of my knees, and we tumble to the mat. The side of his face lands hard against my chest, and my insides suddenly feel like they're on fire.

"Are you okay?" he asks, lifting his head. I feel his cool, minty breath wash over my face as I try to look unaffected and totally badass.

"I ..." hesitating before I can give a normal answer, I say, "I'm fine." I keep my face blank. "Is it my turn?"

A smirk slides across his face, which should be illegal with him being this close to me. "Not yet. You still need to get out of this position. Use your foot like I showed you before. Remember?"

I hook my foot underneath his thigh, trying to maneuver my hips out from under him, but his body is like dead weight against mine, and each and every part of him is over me, pressing me down. I'm grunting, pushing, and clenching my teeth. He just watches, with his smile growing wider and wider.

"What!" I shout, unable to hold back.

He laughs, and it penetrates through my belly. "You're not very patient, are you?" His eyes sparkle playfully.

"I'd be just fine if you didn't have that obnoxious look on your face." I'm fuming. It frustrates me that this one look brings out so many different emotions.

"Sorry," he says, trying to bite back his smile. "Don't rush it. You'll get better results if you're patient."

I know what he's saying is right. Patience has always been a weakness of mine, along with my temper and pride. "Maybe if you stop laughing at me, I could *be* a little more patient," I spit.

"I'm not laughing at you. It's cute. You make these grunting noises, like a little animal."

I know my face is beet red when I start swinging. "I do not! You jerk!"

Holding his hands out in surrender, he says, "Okay, I'm sorry. I'll stop teasing."

I lift my chin. "Say I fight like a goddess, or I'll beat you senseless."

"Fair enough. You fight like a goddess." He cocks a brow. "Can we continue?" I agree to continue, and we alternate positions until both of us are tired and out of steam.

Chapter Thirteen

Beads of sweat slide down the back of my neck by the time I reach my car. After placing a third call into the office, I finally give up and entertain the thought of moving. My Civic chooses to give me hell, so I beat on the steering wheel then violently dig through my purse. When I find what I'm looking for, I punch in a text.

WOULD YOU MIND GIVING ME A RIDE TODAY???

I'm thankful when the reply comes seconds later.

Be there in ten.

I wait in my car until Luke's truck comes into view. It's hot, I'm bitchy, and I really don't want to deal with his shit.

He rolls down the window with a smirk on his face. "Bad day?"

"How'd you guess," I say sarcastically, opening up the passenger door.

After I climb in, he leans over and buckles me in like a child. I let it slide because he looks and smells amazing. "Your text was in all caps."

"I don't even think I meant to do that … must have been my subconscious," I mumble.

He eyes me curiously. "What's going on?"

"Everything." I sigh. "It would take all day for me to explain."

"I'm all ears." The corner of his mouth tips before we make our way out of the complex.

I lean forward so I can feel the cool air blowing toward me. "Well for starters, the A/C in my apartment isn't working right, and it's absolutely miserable. On top of that, my car won't start. Work at Chili's was slow last night so I barely made any money. The bills just keep piling up. So now, I'm just waiting for something else to go wrong. It wouldn't surprise me in the least." I blow a strand of hair out of my eyes, and he chuckles.

"It's not the end of the world." He places his hand on my knee. "I can give you the money to fix your car. Did you talk to management at your complex?"

My eyes drop to his hand, and I mentally kick myself when he moves it. Clearing my throat, I say, "Thanks for offering, but I can't accept that."

He furrows his brows, and I continue.

"As far as management, I've tried multiple times. Nobody answers, and nobody calls back." It's quiet for a minute until we pull up at a red light.

"Reese."

I turn and face him, his golden brown eyes sincere. "I said I'd get your car fixed," he says softly, and I'm entranced by the intensity of his stare. "I'll look at your A/C, too." He grins. "But I can't promise I'll know what I'm doing."

I look at him, blank faced. "But I don't know what's wrong with it, or how much it'll cost." I shake my head. "You know what, don't worry about it," I say, tucking a hair behind my ear. "I'll figure it out."

"Damn it!" he growls, making me flinch. "Would you stop being so stubborn and let me help you?" I'm surprised because I think he's really mad at me.

"What do you mean stubborn?" I narrow my eyes. "For your information, you *are* helping me." Counting on my fingers, I say, "You're giving me rides. You're training me." *You saved me*, I want to say. "What have I done for you?" I ask.

"We're friends." He shrugs. "That's what friends do."

I watch him reach into his pocket and pull out his phone.

"Steve, I need a favor." Luke glances at me with a wry grin. "I have a lady friend who's having problems with her car. You got time to take a look?" I notice a chunk of hair in the back of his head that's sticking up in a funny direction and press my lips together, trying not to laugh.

"It's a Honda Civic," he says before pausing and asking, "Tomorrow?"

I nod when he glances at me.

"That'll work." He looks at me again and furrows his brows. "Yep. No problem." Narrowing his eyes, he adds, "I'll drive her around." He watches me carefully.

His words have me fidgeting in my seat. The thought of driving around with Luke makes me nervous, and I'm pretty sure he's aware of this fact.

When I meet his eyes, the cocky bastard winks at me. "See you then, bud." He puts his phone away then taps on the steering wheel. "See."

I arch a brow. "See what?"

"Nothin' to worry about." Reaching over, he squeezes the lower part of my thigh. His hand feels like it belongs there, but if I act like I notice, he'll move it. So I don't.

"We'll see about that," I murmur.

His brows lift. "He said it may take a couple days, but he'll do it. He needs to find out what's wrong first." He shrugs his shoulders. "It might be an easy fix, like the battery or alternator. If that's the case, it shouldn't take long at all."

"I can probably get help from Gia if it turns out to be a bigger problem."

"Good." He nods. "You've got both of us then."

I lean back against the headrest and sigh. "Thank you."

He nods then asks, "Do you work at Chili's this week?"

"No, I already worked my shifts."

"See …" He smiles. "All taken care of."

We arrive at work, and the girls are already geared up, anxiously waiting the lesson.

"Hi Luke!" several of them shout excitedly.

I place my hands on my hips, faking offense. "What about me?"

They all giggle, some of them blushing. "Hi Reese!" *My goodness. Does he have this effect on everyone?*

"You're starting to make me jealous," I mumble, swatting him with the back of my hand.

"Ouch!" He flinches playfully.

My mouth drops. "Don't believe him, girls. He knows how to put on a show." I spot Ally watching me with a funny expression, so I make my way over and ask, "What's with the look, Miss Ally?"

Her brows move up and down before her eyes drift to Luke then back to me. "You know …" She grins. "You two came here together."

I lean down and whisper, "You silly girl. My car broke down, and I needed a ride." When she glances toward the other girls they cover their mouths and snicker. *I see, so they're all in on it.*

"I like your outfit," Taylor interrupts before Maddy and Rylee agree. I drop my gaze to the fitted pink top and stretchy charcoal shorts—an outfit that Luke won't be 'comfortable' with. My cheeks heat as my eyes flick to his, and a lazy smile stretches across his face. Then he scratches his head and looks away.

"Okay girls. Reese and I are going to demonstrate a little of what we did last week. Do you remember what we practiced?" The girls nod their heads, sitting side by side with their legs crossed.

"This time I'm going to throw Reese down on the mat, and she's going to try to get out from underneath me by flipping me over."

I turn and look at him, clearly annoyed, and he flashes his signature grin, dimples and all. I suck at this. He knows I can't get out of it, and every time I try, I have to deal with him smirking like he won the damn lottery.

"You ready?" he asks with a look I love to hate.

Lifting my chin in defiance, I say, "Ready when you are."

Then, he tackles me. We land hard on the mat, so I wait for an open opportunity. I savor my strength, trying to stay patient as the weight of his body lies over me. His arms are pinning me down, but I get my footing in a secure place. I don't look at him. It's too distracting, and when I'm finally able to maneuver my hips, it works.

Our hearts pound frantically while we both try to catch our breaths. I stare at him in shock as I lie on top of him.

"Kiss him!" one of the girls shouts.

I lift my eyes to meet his, and they sparkle before a devilish smirk appears.

"You did it," he says softly.

I clear my throat, quickly climbing off of him. I don't want to do something stupid like grab his face and kiss him then run my fingers through his sexy hair.

"You did good!" Ally says excitedly.

I smile before my brows knit together, confused. *Did he let me do that?*

The girls practiced on each other the rest of the period. Luckily after several tries, most of them seemed to have it down.

Chapter Fourteen

"I have no idea what I'm doing." Luke frowns, after spending and hour and a half on my A/C.

"At least you tried." I shrug. "Which is more than I can say for the management." He purses his lips, looking down at his hands, which are now covered in grease."

"Sorry about that," I say, before pointing him in the direction of the bathroom. I quickly check my reflection in a nearby mirror and jump when a loud noise startles me. When I make my way into the kitchen, I see Luke's phone buzzing on the counter. I reach over and answer it, without even thinking, then look around to see if I'm caught.

"Luke?" I hear a female voice say.

Squeezing my eyes shut. *Damn! What am I doing?* "Um he's busy," I reply, then nervously glance toward the bathroom.

Her voice sounds a little bothered when she asks, "Who's this?"

At first, I debate not telling her then finally give up. "This is Reese," I pause, "I'm his friend."

"Oh ..." she says after a moment of silence.

"Can I take a message?" I ask in a fake chipper tone.

"S-sure," she stutters. "Can you tell him to call Lauren?"

Why am I not surprised?

"And tell him it's important," she adds just as Luke walks out of the bathroom. Glancing toward the counter before his eyes move back to his phone, he cocks a brow.

"Wait, Lauren he can talk now. Here he is." I hand it over, embarrassed to look at him.

"Hey," he answers.

When I lift my lashes he's looking directly at me, narrowing his eyes. I shuffle back and forth afraid I got him in trouble. Then he makes his way out the front door, leaving me alone in my kitchen.

It takes several long minutes before he walks back into my apartment. I occupy my time with a book, but I startle when his phone slams on my counter. Very slowly, he turns around looking the most pissed I've ever seen him. "Do me a favor," he snaps. "Don't answer my phone."

The embarrassment I was feeling earlier turns to boiling rage. How dare he talk to me like that! *Screw privacy.* "I was trying to help!" I yell. "Don't talk to me like I'm a child!"

"Then stop acting like one," he spits.

"You're an asshole!"

He takes a step back, watching me, then sighs. "Look, It's not your fault." He runs a palm over his face resigning. "There's a lot of stuff going on—stuff you don't know about—that you don't need to know about," he finishes. "I shouldn't have yelled at you."

I fold my arms, arching a brow. "And?"

"And I'm sorry," he replies with a soft chuckle.

Tilting my head, I ask, "What's so funny?" I really want to know, but he just laughs harder.

"I'm waiting for the smoke to come out of your ears."

"Really?" I ask, placing my hands on my hips. "Do you know how bad I want to hurt you right now?"

He nods his head, and I'm pretty sure I see tears. I playfully swing at his shoulder, and he grabs my wrist then taunts me. "Is that all you've got."

I bring my face right up to his and whisper, "You infuriate me." I swing at him with the other arm, and he grabs that wrist as well.

"Good," he replies.

I clench my teeth at his cockiness. "Wipe that stupid smirk off your face, boy." I stick out my leg trying to trip him. "Let go of me. You jerk!"

"If I do, are you going to attack me?" he asks, cocking a brow.

"Of course I am!" I hiss.

Leaning down, he whispers, "Then sorry princess, I'm not gonna let go."

My body ignites with adrenaline, as I twist and turn under his grasp. I start kicking him in the leg, and he flinches before wrestling me to the ground, stretching my arms above my head. His grip around my wrists becomes tighter, stronger. It doesn't hurt, still I try to buck him off. The electricity igniting between us makes me instantly aware of every part of him that's touching me. When I feel his arousal, I go still. My chest rises and falls, as I stare into those eyes.

Hunger flashes his gaze, and the corner of his mouth tilts. He softly says, "You keep moving around like that, we're gonna have a problem." His eyes fall to my lips.

I'm too caught up in our chemistry to care about my traitorous blush. Our lips are an inch apart, and my heart races, as I wonder if he'll kiss me. He slowly rolls off—disappointing me—before he breaks the silence.

"It's been a long time since I've had a good laugh." He stands then holds out a hand. "Sorry it was at your expense." After he pulls me up I clear my throat, quickly turning away. I'm terrified that my expression will betray me.

"I'll get your A/C fixed. I'm gonna call around," he says.

I look over my shoulder. "No way. You're not going to pay for that, too." I turn around and shrug. "I'll just wait for maintenance … it's fine."

"Seriously woman, you're driving me crazy!"

I place my hands on my hips and give him my best glare. "Why? Because I don't want to depend on a man to support me?"

"Aw, would you just shut up already?" he groans then adds, "It's hot in here. I'm dying!" Pulling his shirt away from his body, he starts fanning himself. He's right, it is hot, but I don't know what else to tell him.

"Thank you for trying to fix it. I really appreciate it." I grab his keys and phone then hand them to him. "I can take it from here."

He takes a few steps closer and lifts his brows. "Why don't you come stay with me until you get it fixed?"

Now *that* totally caught me by surprise. "Stay with you?" I tuck a strand of hair behind my ear and ask, "Wouldn't that upset Lauren?"

A wry smirk slowly slides on his face. "Lauren won't mind," he says confidently.

I find it hard to believe him, but I'd be lying if I said this wasn't tempting, for several reasons I don't want to name.

"Thanks for offering," I say. "Maybe I'll take you up on that." I bite back a smile when he flashes his dimpled grin. "I'll try maintenance again tomorrow and see if I hear anything."

He shrugs his shoulders. "It makes sense since I'm going to be driving you around anyway.

Is he trying to talk me into it? God, he's so confusing.

"Oh! Speaking of driving, can you take me to the work party Friday?"

He tilts his head. "Yeah, isn't it supposed to be at some club?"

"Yes. That was Kyle's idea," I murmur. "Several of the guys talked about changing it up over the usual dinner party. Majority won. I think it increases their chances of getting lucky."

"I see," he says, arching a brow. "Are you using a fake ID?"

I blush. "Yes, but it'll only be the second time I've used it," I say, grinning. "I'm not a lush or anything."

His eyes dance and he flashes that sideways smile. "I never said you were."

I shrug. "Anyway, I'm sure it'll be fun, but I'll let you go home now."

He nods then jingles his keys in his hand before he turns to walk away.

"You're sure you don't mind giving me a ride?" I yell out again, still feeling the weight of his earlier rejection.

He looks over his shoulder and shouts, "Not at all." He holds up his keys. "I'm your designated driver."

Chapter Fifteen

"This class sucks," I say, glancing at the paper on my left. It has a giant letter A scrawled on it in bright red pen. "How do you do that?" I ask Luke.

"He only gives a pass or fail grade. I can help you both if you need it."

Gia grabs my arm then leans all the way across me. "That would be great. What about today after school?" Flicking her gaze toward me, she says, "We can all go to her apartment."

"No way." I lean back and arch a brow. "I do everything I can to stay away from there. My air conditioner still isn't working."

"I told you to stay with me, stubborn ass," Luke growls.

"He told you what?" Gia whispers, but it's loud enough that Luke can hear. I shake my head, begging her to drop it. But she sits back and says, "I would say you could stay with me, but you'd have to sleep on the floor." She shrugs. "I have company." I glare at her, knowing she's full of shit. "Don't you remember?" she asks, demonstrating her acting abilities.

"No, I don't remember," I answer skeptically and notice Luke chewing on his pen, smirking. Part of me hopes it leaks all over his mouth, but in real life, those things only happen to me. "Careful," I say as his grin grows wider.

"You guys can study at my place," Gia says. "I don't live as close, but it's only about ten minutes more." The bell rings, and we all head for the exit.

Luke nods. "I can do that."

"Works for me, I don't have a car." We make our way to the parking lot, and I glance at Luke. "I'll ... um ... ride with Gia." She grabs my wrist and squeezes it, before I walk to the other side of her car, quickly getting in when she unlocks it.

As soon as I sit down, she whacks me with the back of her hand.

"Ouch! What was that for?"

She rolls down the window and shouts, "Luke, just follow me." She whips her head around to me, adding, "You really know how to play hard to get, don't you?"

My mouth drops. "What? He's had plenty of opportunities to make a move. He hasn't. If he wanted me, he would've made one already."

"Oh, he wants you," she says. "Anybody can see that."

"How?" I arch a brow. "How do you know?"

She snorts. "By the way he looks at you! C'mon! It's totally obvious!"

"Look Gia," I say. "The other night, I thought he was going to kiss me. I could see it in his eyes." The memory of his arousal flashes through my head. "I could feel that he was thinking about it." Tucking my hair behind my ear, I add, "And when I say feel, I mean *feel*. But then ... he just sort of rolled off of me."

She turns the radio all the way down, and asks, "So he was lying on top of you when this *almost kiss* happened?" Her eyes look hopeful.

I lick my lips. "Yes. We were in my apartment."

She nods. "In your apartment ... I see. And when you say, *you could feel that he was thinking about it*, do you mean ... he was hard?" She arches a brow, pressing her lips together in a tight smirk.

I instantly blush, knowing exactly what she's getting at. Clearing my throat, I say, "Very."

"Reese Savannah Johnson!" She gasps. "You've just felt your first hard on!"

"Shh. Okay," I hiss. "Stop yelling! This isn't a public matter!"

"Oh, that's right," she says. "He might hear us from his car." I figure she has a point, and start laughing before she joins me in hysterical laughter. When Gia catches her breath she says, "Well, if he was hard, then you're right; he was definitely thinking about it, and probably more." She tilts her head. "Maybe he wants you to make the first move."

I think about it then say, "He doesn't seem like the type. He's sort of a take charge kind of guy."

"Yeah, but he's different with you."

"Not really," I murmur. "Besides, when it comes to men, I have no clue what I'm doing. With my luck, I'd do something wrong."

She purses her lips. "Maybe it's time to make him jealous."

"And how am I going to do that?" I scoff.

"Chill out and listen. This could be very beneficial," she looks at me pointedly. "You said you have a work party coming up, right?"

I arch a brow. "Yeah, so."

"You guys are going to a club?"

"Yesss," I draw out the word, slowly nodding my head. "Luke is driving me. What's your point?"

"My point is, find some hot guys at the club, and dance with them." She shrugs. "It'll be like a test. If he has feelings for you, he won't like it. In fact, it'll probably drive him mad." She grins. "I've seen it with other alpha males like him. They can't handle it."

"Okay. And what if your plan is worthless, and I'm stuck dancing with a bunch of horny men I could care less about?"

"Trust me. He'll do something to keep them away. Who knows? Maybe the only person you'll end up dancing with is him." She wiggles her brows suggestively.

"Why don't I like this plan?"

"I'm really not sure, because it's brilliant," she says confidently. "And it's going to work."

"Ugh." I throw my head in my hands. "I'll need a few drinks if you expect me to dance with random guys."

"Just be careful lightweight. We don't want drunk Reese to come out and play." She tilts her head. "Then again, maybe we do." The corner of her mouth slants.

I whip my head around. "Hey! You've only seen me drunk once."

"Yeah, I know. Remember?" She lifts her brows, and I press my lips together to keep from arguing. "Just saying."

Chapter Sixteen

Luke

"What's she doing out there?" I ask, nodding my head in Reese's direction. She's on the dance floor—swinging her hips from side to side—with some random loser standing right up behind her.

Kyle chuckles. "I think she's trying to piss you off."

"She's succeeding," I respond, unable to tear my eyes away.

"Look at your straw." He grins. "You've been chewing on it like candy."

"Habit," I say back then take it out of my mouth and grab another.

"You want to dance, handsome?" a tall blonde purrs into my ear. She's got her tits pouring out of her shirt, and it's obvious she's braless. Kyle freezes beside me as I eye her from head to toe. The only woman I'm interested in is the feisty little brunette on the dance floor.

"I'm busy." I flick my gaze back to Reese. "But Kyle over here would love to."

Reese is wearing a sexy little dress that clings to every part of her body. I had to blink away the images that came to my mind the second she opened the door.

"He thinks he's getting laid," Kyle says after we watch some loser press his mouth to Reese's ear.

"Not going to happen," I growl back, ready to hit someone.

"You don't think?"

Giving him a lethal glare, I tell him, "I'm her ride home, and I'm pretty sure she's not that kind of girl." Cocking a brow, I ask, "Aren't you supposed to be with boobs?"

He gives a half grin. "She turned me down, man. Shit, she was fine."

"I tried," I mumble.

"Thanks for tryin'," he replies before his eyes focus back on Reese. "He's going to be disappointed, cuz her body language says he's getting lucky." Shaking his head back and forth, he adds, "She's got killer legs dude, and that dress is ..." I swat him in the back of the head, and he flies forward. "Ouch!" he yells. "What the fuck, man? I didn't say I was taking her home!"

"You wouldn't have a chance," I snort.

"Yeah, I know. Even if I did, I'd be competing with the big, bad Luke Ryann, who would kick my ass in the process," he says. "It's clear that you're in love with her."

I choke on my straw and turn to him. "How many drinks have you had?"

"I don't know, like five or six," he pauses then asks, "Why?"

"Cuz you're starting to get on my nerves."

After the music changes tempo, Reese makes her way in our direction. The guy who's trailing behind is staring at her ass, and I'm about to lose it.

"You ready?" I ask her.

She grins and looks over her shoulder. "Actually we're getting another drink."

The happy look on her face bugs the shit out of me. I stare down the prick as I lean in close to her ear, letting him know she's important to me, but also marking my territory. "Are you sure you need another one?" *Mmm, I love the way she smells.* When I pull away, she furrows her brows.

"What's that supposed to mean?"

"It means I think you've had too much," I answer. Sure, I'm being a dick, but it's the truth, and she needs to hear it. I'm trying really hard not to earn myself a lawsuit, but if she keeps this up, shit's about to go down.

She looks at me quizzically. "Are you mad or something?"

"No, I'm not mad." *Irritated, definitely.* "You've just reached your limit, and I'm not going to stand back and let this dildo take advantage of you."

She puts her hands on her hips, ready to give me attitude. *Bring it on, princess.* "So we're back to that now, huh? You treating me like a child?"

I shrug. "Only when you act like one, sweetheart."

"Says who?"

I take a step closer. "Says me," I say, pointing to myself.

She stands on the tips of her toes, trying to get in my face, but I don't back down. "Oh yeah, how's that?"

My face is less than an inch from hers when I say, "First of all, your demeanor has completely changed. You've tipped back several drinks since we've been here, and you don't seem to mind that *Johnny Dildo* over here's putting his hands on you." I pause before continuing, "And staring at your ass!"

The guy chuckles.

"Something funny?"

His grin quickly disappears. "No sir."

My eyes fall back on her when she walks around me, stumbling her way to the bar. The guy follows with his hand on the small of her back. He's got a lot of nerve. I'll give him that. I guess I'm going to have to scare the hell out of him.

"The tension between the two of you is sick," Kyle says, distracting me.

I give a short laugh. "You think?"

The corner of his mouth slopes. "It's like a contest. Who can piss the other off more," he says, very matter of fact.

"I'll admit, I like to piss her off," I grin. "Don't know why, but I do."

"She likes to piss you off, too." We both laugh at that.

"Hell yeah she does, and she's good at it." I put another straw in my mouth and contemplate that for a second. "Why is that, I wonder?"

He looks at me like I'm insane. "Isn't it obvious?"

I lift my brows, waiting for him to continue.

"It's passion." He bobs his head. "Get it over with already."

For once, I have no idea how to respond to that.

After another hour of talking myself out of putting Johnny Dildo in a body bag, he gives up. To my amusement, Reese wasn't interested in what he was offering. Now she's dancing with a group of girls, and I finally feel like I can relax.

"Will you keep an eye on her while I hit the head?"

"Uh … sure." Kyle responds. "She's gonna be pissed if she finds out you just asked me that."

"She's drunk man. You think I give a shit?"

"Hell no!" He grins.

It takes less than two minutes to take a leak and make my way back to our spot, but Kyle isn't there, so I flick my gaze to the dance floor, narrowing my eyes on a couple straight ahead. *You've got to be kidding me.*

"Don't kill me, man. I didn't want to mess with that dude. He's like twice my size," Kyle says, instantly blocking my view.

"Move," I growl. "And shut up."

I watch them sway from side to side as she sips on another drink. I wouldn't be surprised if she puked or passed out from all the alcohol. I've tried to consider her feelings—tried not to treat her like a child—but he's pressing himself against her, and I'm drawing the line.

"Luke!" Logan grins. "What's up buddy? Good to see you here, man!"

Keeping my eyes on Reese, I ignore him. "It's late. I'm tired, let's go."

"You two know each other?" Logan asks as Reese looks back and forth between us.

When she speaks, it's apparent she's drunk. "What's your problem? I'm dancing. You should try it." She's the only person I'd want to dance with. But I can't, not when she looks like that.

I grab her arm. "You're drunk. We're leaving."

She jerks it away. "I'm not going anywhere with you! I said I'm dancing!"

"Oh yeah? Well the party is over, and I'm your ride. Let's go."

Logan places his hands on her shoulders. "I don't know what's up with you, buddy, but the lady says she doesn't want to go." Dropping his gaze to Reese, he continues, "I can take you home if you need a ride." His voice is soft; it's the voice he uses when he's trying to get laid.

"The hell you will!" I shout, inches from his face.

He puts his hand on the small of her back. "Calm down man. Let the lady decide who she's going home with. You don't get to have them all."

"You have one second to move your hand before I break it," I say calmly, meaning every single word.

Understanding flashes in his eyes before he backs off, carefully watching me.

"Not this one Logan. You got me?"

The corner of his mouth angles. "Yeah," he answers. "I think I do."

I drop my gaze to Reese and notice her bright red cheeks. She's more pissed than I've ever seen her. Blowing a piece of hair out of her eyes she says, "I'm not going with you, Luke!"

"You're coming with me, even if I have to carry you."

Her mouth drops. "Why are you being like this?"

"So you enjoy being molested by strangers when you're intoxicated? I'll have to take note of that."

She slaps me. It stings, but I don't flinch or break eye contact. I don't care that I'm pissing her off. I want to get her home safe, far away from here. I take her by the hand and drag her toward Kyle and the rest of the group. Like a spoiled child, she fights me the whole way.

"We're leaving," I tell them.

"I want to stay," she yells, glaring at me. "And of course I don't enjoy having a total stranger rub all over me. In fact I think it's disgusting! But I don't need you intervening. I can take care of myself."

"You don't look so good Reese, you should probably get going," Kyle tells her. I give a small nod of gratitude as she huffs behind me. We make our way to the parking lot, and she's running her mouth.

"Let go of my arm! You can't make me leave!"

"If you keep fighting me, I'm gonna do something you're not gonna like."

"I was having fun! He offered to give me a ride anyway!"

"Believe me, your fun was about to end pretty quickly."

"You're just jealous!"

"You're right, I've always wanted to be groped by two dildos in a club." She yanks her arm out of my hand and marches back toward the entrance.

"That's it," I say, following her. "You give me no other choice." I pick her up and throw her over my shoulder, sticking my hand right on her ass, giving it a squeeze, just to make her angrier."

"Put me down you pervert!"

"Nope."

"Why are you doing this?" she yells.

"Because I care about you."

"Ha! Well, I don't care about you," she scoffs, punching the middle of my back.

She eases up a little when I finally get her in my truck. We pull out of the parking lot and head to her apartment in complete and utter silence.

"I think I'm going to be sick," she grumbles against the window.

"Do you need me to pull over?"

"Not yet. I'll let you know."

"Five minutes." I pat her on the knee. "I'm hurrying." She stares out the windshield and doesn't respond.

We finally make it to her complex without any accidents. I watch her reach under the passenger seat, frantically feeling around her feet.

"What are you looking for?"

"My keys," she gasps. "I locked them in my apartment."

"Do you have another set somewhere?"

She shakes her head. "No, only at the front office."

I purse my lips taking a look at the clock. "You could always come home with me. I'd bring you back in the morning."

She fidgets nervously.

"Are you feeling okay?" It's been about an hour since she had her last drink. If she were going to hurl, it would happen about now.

"I still feel the alcohol, but as long as I don't think about it, I should be fine." She grabs her phone and says, "Let me call Gia and ask if I can stay there." I watch her tap in the numbers.

"It's Reese, call me as soon as you get this. I'm locked out of my apartment." Glancing at me, she adds, "I'm in the parking lot with Luke. Hurry. Call me back." Snapping her phone shut, she frowns.

Unable to hold back my amusement, I say, "How many personalities do you have?"

Her brows lift. "Me?"

I look around the cab of the truck. "Yes you. I saw a side of you tonight I never thought I'd see, completely unlike the girl I know."

Biting her nails, she mumbles, "How?"

I chuckle. "Promise you're not gonna slap me?"

She slowly nods her head, eyeing me warily. "I promise."

"Right now, sitting with you in my car, I see your vulnerable side. It's a side I've become used to. Right there." I point. "The color in your cheeks, I've seen it many times. It's a part of this *you* I'm used to."

Turning away, she asks, "Then what's so different?"

"Tonight at the bar," I pause, shaking my head, "you were somebody else."

"Is that a bad thing?" She waits, as she plays with the hem of her dress.

I cock a brow. "I'd say both good and bad, if you want me to be totally honest."

She throws her head in her hands. "Tell me the bad first. I already have an idea."

"Are you going to yell at me or start swinging if you don't like my answer?" She peeks through her fingers and shakes her head no.

"Promise?"

"I promise! Damn it! Just tell me already!"

"All right, here goes. The bad, is that you were acting like a spoiled child who couldn't get her way. Not to mention, you had two or three pairs of unfamiliar hands rubbing all over your body, which you seemed to thoroughly enjoy." She opens her mouth to interrupt. "Can I finish?" I ask.

"Oh God," she moans. "Go ahead."

"In your defense, you could blame it on the alcohol. It just caught me off guard since you freak out whenever I touch you, and I've never touched you like that."

I reach over and brush her bright red cheek with my thumb. "Can I continue with the good, or is there something you wanted to say?"

"You can, um … continue," she answers, clearing her throat.

"As for the good …" I grin. "Well, that's easy." I let my eyes roam over her, slowly lifting my gaze back up. "Your dress."

She tilts her head. "What do you mean?"

I wink. "I mean you're wearing it."

Her mouth drops, and she playfully swats me with her hand.

"Ouch! I'm being nice. Why are you hitting me? And you made a promise."

"You know why. That's the only good thing you could come up with?"

I shrug. "Yeah, you were a pain in the ass tonight, and every time I see you, you're dressed for work. When you opened your door wearing a dress that fits you like … well … like that, and your hair was all up … like that … I just …" Hesitating to find the right words, wondering where I'm taking this, I pause.

"You just what?" she asks softly.

"I just … think you look beautiful," I finally say, feeling like I never should have opened my mouth. "Look, we're both tired, and it's getting late." I sigh. "Why don't you stay with me?"

She bites her lip, getting all shy on me, and the color comes back to her cheeks.

"That didn't come out right … I'm saying, why don't you just stay at my place. I'll bring you back in the morning."

"Are you sure?"

"Yeah, I'm sure."

She hesitates. "Do you have room? I mean, where will I sleep?" She looks nervous as hell, and I can't help the grin that spreads across my face.

"In my bed of course." I look straight ahead, while she shuffles in the seat beside me. I cock a brow. "I'm teasing you. I'll take the couch."

She grins. "Ha ha, very funny."

"I couldn't help myself."

We're almost to my place when Reese breaks the silence saying, "I don't want you to think this is something I do all the time—that I go to the bars regularly or sleep around … because I don't."

"I never thought that, but thanks for letting me know."

"And I could count on one hand how many times I've been drunk."

I snort. "Well that explains a lot—all the more reason to get you out of there."

"I'm glad you did. Thank you," she says, looking out her window as we pull into the driveway, and I can tell she means it.

"I'd do it again." I reach over and squeeze her hand.

"I know you would."

Chapter Seventeen

Luke

"So this is it," I tell her, watching her stumble her way into my kitchen. "There's not much to it."

She grips the large island to balance herself and gazes at all the modern décor. "I think it's great."

I chuckle. "Maybe you should take those things off." I glance at her heels.

"You don't like my stilettos?"

Running a hand through my hair, I reply, "I think they're sexy as hell, until you start stumbling around in them." She blushes then slowly takes them off.

"You're blushing again." I smirk. "Don't get all embarrassed. I've been there … many times. Trust me."

Her eyes fall on the granite as she brushes her fingers along the edge. "That's not why I'm blushing," she says, gently biting on her lip. "I'm blushing because you said my shoes are sexy." She lifts her lashes.

I could take the look she just gave me a couple of different ways—both of them lead to reminding myself which head to listen to. "Come on. I'll show you around." I make my way down the hall, and she follows closely behind.

"So you like the modern look," she quips, glancing at what little décor I have. I'm not in to harboring junk, and I don't like to deal with clutter.

"You could say that." I shrug. "I like it simple ... clean."

She taps a finger against her lips, playfully arching a brow. "Interesting. I wouldn't expect that from a bachelor."

The corner of my mouth tips, and I lean against the wall crossing my arms. "Really now?"

She nods her head and smiles before she continues, "I'd expect a mess, clothes all over the place, and dishes piled high in the sink."

"That's what you expected to find here?"

"No. Not from you. You're not like the typical bachelor." She smiles then opens up the door to the weight room. Her mouth drops. "Wow! Why do you even go to the gym when you've got all this?" she asks, looking over her shoulder.

I glance at all the weights, the cardio equipment, and the heavy bag. "Working out at home gets old. Besides, I like to change things up."

Still holding her hand, she leads me toward my room at the end of the hall. "This is your room?"

I nod before she quickly reaches back, letting down all of her hair. I clench my jaw watching as she makes her way over to my bed.

"Come here," she says softly before lying all the way back on the mattress.

I hesitate; feeling like a virgin, I sit on the side farthest away from her. Seeing Reese lying across my bed is having an effect on me. I'd be lying if I said I didn't like it … and that could be a problem.

"What's wrong?" she asks, her brows knitting together.

I groan and place my head in my hands until I hear her begin to laugh. Snapping my head up I ask, "Are you laughing at me?"

Her eyes glisten in a fit of giggles, and she covers her mouth and says, "Yes," in a high-pitched squeal she could barely get out. She's rolling around on the bed, now unable to control it. I don't know if it's because she's tanked or if I'm really *that* amusing.

"I'm glad you find me funny," I say, before I'm right there laughing along with her.

When we're finally able to contain ourselves, she scoots closer. "It's just that, when you're nervous, you do this thing where you tap your foot like this." She taps her foot like she's having some sort of seizure, obviously exaggerating. "You also tug on your hair like this … she shows me then wipes away the rest of her tears.

"Is that so?" I tease, cocking a brow. Her eyes sparkle when I bring my face inches from hers. "And why would I be nervous?"

She only answers with a shrug.

I tilt my head closer to her. "So now you're not going to tell me?" Reaching over, I tickle her side. "You think you've got me figured out?" I whisper.

She squeals, "More than you know," trying her best attempt to squirm away from my fingers.

"Really?" I chuckle into her ear, letting her breathe.

She pulls the hair out of her face smoothing over the evidence of my assault. "I sure do."

"Okay." I nod. "Please, humor me. What else have you figured out?"

Her smile fades, and her eyes fall to the floor. I'm worried I said something that offended her. It happens all the time. "I said something wrong. Didn't I?"

She lifts her lashes. Her green eyes gaze into mine. "Why didn't you tell me?"

I arch a brow, confused by whatever the hell she's talking about. "Tell you what?" I search her face carefully. She's biting her lip, trying her best not to cry.

"I'm okay," she sniffles. "I'm probably crying cuz I'm drunk."

I take her face in my hands so she'll look at me, feeling like a complete ass. "Whatever it is I did, I never meant to hurt you."

She gives a short laugh then tucks her hair behind her ear. "You didn't hurt me. I'm just having a hard time getting this out."

"Okay." I wipe a tear from her face. "Then tell me why you're crying? I'm not very good with tears."

"I'm trying to tell you," she replies, inhaling a deep breath then slowly releasing it, and I reach out and tuck another strand of hair behind her ear, just because I want to.

Meeting my eyes, she says, "I could never thank you enough for what you did that day, six years ago, in my bedroom."

I stare at her, blank faced, not knowing what to say, and she continues as if she didn't just drop a bomb on me.

"I've known for a while, and I don't know if I can ever forgive myself for how I've treated you. Ever since the first day I met you ... you always tried to protect me." She grins. "And you did. Can you imagine what could have happened if you hadn't been there?" Her brows lift.

I run a hand through my hair, confused about why she didn't say anything. "I don't want to imagine, to be honest. I should have gone ahead and shot him when I had the chance. At least then he'd be dead and gone."

"You did the right thing," she says softly. "Besides, you'd be locked up in prison." She takes my hand and adds, "Who would come to my rescue then?"

Glancing at our joined hands I ask, "When did you figure it out?" I swallow and continue, "How long have you known."

The corner of her mouth tips. "The first time I saw you at the gym, there was something familiar about you, but I just couldn't place it." She sniffs. "Then it slapped me right in the face when I caught you staring at my scar. That's when it all came together." She shrugs. "Your eyes gave it away."

I gaze at the small scar beneath her brow, remembering when she got it. "You were bleeding," I say, lightly brushing my thumb over the scar, then softly graze her cheek with my knuckles. "I'm sorry."

She watches me carefully, then says, "Don't apologize for my father ... or for Ronald. Don't you dare."

Sighing, I lay on my back. "I left you." Resting my eyes, I add, "After everything that happened with your father. I left you."

"Are you serious?"

"Hell yeah I'm serious! I left you to fend for yourself." I sit up and stare at her.

She watches me carefully. "Luke, you were what ... sixteen? You were just a child. You didn't really have a choice! Plus, you did come back, right at the time I needed you most."

Memories of that night start flashing through my mind. Pam and Jim had gone on one of their trips. I was nineteen and living on my own. They had asked me to keep an eye on the house, and take care of the dogs. "When I heard the screams coming from your place, it was like an out of body experience." I scratch my head and gaze at the floor. "One minute I'm making a sandwich, and the next, I'm a second away from blowing the prick's head off." Shaking my head, I add, "I don't remember anything in between, just that I had to get you out of there."

"And you did," she says before she bites on her lip then adds, "This is sort of embarrassing, but I'm going to go ahead and say it while I have the nerve." She inhales a sharp breath then slowly lets it out. "And I swear I will kill Gia if this turns out badly," she grumbles.

"Alcohol makes you brave." I smirk, nudging her with my shoulder. "And honest."

She blushes. "Okay, here it goes." Glancing at her lap, she begins, "I've sort of had a crush on you since the first night you came to my window ... the night when my father gave me this scar." She pulls at the hem of her dress, lifting her eyes to meet mine. "That was nine years ago."

Those words were not what I expected. "You were just a kid," is all I'm able to say.

She furrows her brows then murmurs, "So were you."

"Yeah, but a five year age difference is a big deal when you're a kid. Running a hand through my hair, I add, "It was an innocent crush, and I just happened to be there." If she's going where I think she's going, I can't give her what she wants.

I stand up and walk to the other side of the room, needing to put some distance between us. Regardless of what I feel, I'll never be able to act on it. Hearing her say she shares the same feelings makes everything more complicated.

Watching from over her shoulder before turning to face me, she replies, "Maybe it did start out as an innocent crush." She shrugs. "Maybe it was because you saved me. But what does that have to do with now?"

I can't look in her eyes. I don't want to see the hurt that I'm going to put there. So I focus my gaze behind her as I feel her step closer. Closing my eyes before opening them I say, "It's late, let's get you to bed."

"Why are you acting like this?" She places her hand on my face, and I lower my gaze to meet hers. "You're nervous. I can tell." The corner of her mouth slants. I have to force myself not to hold her down and kiss her. "You're a good guy, Luke, and I promise I'm not drunk." Her eyes go soft. "I meant every word I said."

My thoughts conflict, staring deep into her beautiful green eyes. I lean down and press my forehead against hers, then breath in her sweet scent. "You don't understand," I say gently. "It's not safe … for you to be with me."

She pulls away, arching a brow in amusement. "Not safe?" She grins. "Nothing makes me feel more safe than when I'm with you." She reaches up and gently runs her fingers through my hair then takes a couple steps back. "I want to be with you, Luke, more than I've ever wanted anything in my entire life." Her movements are careful and slow when she unzips her dress and I watch it fall to the floor.

I focus on the lacey black material and the most beautiful body I've ever seen. I'm as hard as a rock, and can't bring myself to tear my eyes away. It takes every ounce of my being not to reach out and touch her.

"I want you to make love to me," she says in small voice. She's just as nervous as I am, biting down on her lip, and I notice her cheeks beginning to turn pink.

My protective side kicks in—an attempt to save her from me. "What the hell are you doing?" I growl, frustrated in more ways than one. My brain has taken a vacation, but my physical side is on high alert. She's only a few feet away, looking sexy as hell in nothing but her bra and panties.

Crossing her arms defensively, she says, "What does it look like I'm doing?"

I groan and run my hands over my face. "Reese."

In that moment, something flashes in her eyes. "Oh my God. You don't want me!" she gasps.

"Reese, just let me try to explain …"

"No Luke, I get it. Really." Her gaze drops to the ground, then letting out a small sarcastic laugh, she says, "I don't know how to do sexy." She backs up, covering herself with her hands.

I grind my teeth in irritation, roughly tugging on my hair. She has no idea how sexy she is. *I don't want her? Is she crazy? Damn it! I'm fucked!*

"I mean … was I … was I turning you off?" she asks. "It's just that I … I've never …"

Unable to take anymore, I cut her off, backing her against the wall. Placing my hands on either side of her head, I cage her in. Leaning down, I place my nose at the base of her throat, breathing in her scent, as I slowly trail my way to her temple. "Do you have any idea what you do to me Reese?" I say softly.

She answers on a whimper when my lips graze the spot below her ear. Gripping the back of her neck, I ask, "Is that what you think? That seeing you like this, hearing you say you want me is turning me off?" She gives a small nod, and I smile at the feel of her racing pulse. "Mmm, you're killing me, you know that?"

"Ye-yes-ss," she stutters.

"Knowing how this affects you …" Grazing my fingers down her neck then across her jaw, she trembles. "Mmm, it's doing crazy things to me." I brush my thumb over the tiny bumps appearing on her arm. "Remind me," I say, quietly chuckling, letting her feel my desire for her. "What was it you were saying?" When I pull away, everything happens so fast.

She grabs my face and brings her mouth to mine, kissing me hard. Without a single thought in mind, I'm kissing her back, moving my hands to her hips as she frantically rips the buttons off my shirt. I feel her nails dig deep into my back, bringing an animalistic growl out of me. I lift her up, and she wraps her legs around my waist, straddling me. One of my hands tangles into her hair while the other grips firmly on her thigh. The kiss deepens, and my tongue continues to devour her. All I can think about is how she tastes against my mouth, how I want more, need more, can't get enough of her.

"Please Luke," she gasps. "You're the … I've never." Between our kissing and trying to catch a breath, she can't get the words out.

I move my lips to her neck. "Say it. Tell me what you want."

"I want you to be my first."

Her what? The words hit me like a bucket of cold water. With no time to think, I gently pull on her bottom lip and carry her into the bathroom. *What was I thinking?* Losing my grip on one of her thighs, I reach across to open the shower door.

In one swift movement, I set her inside and turn on the water, backing away as I watch her. *Man, she's pissed.*

"What are you doing?" she yells. There's water dripping down her face, continuing to her bra and panties.

I feel terrible, but she's been drinking, and there's no way I'm taking her virginity tonight. "Getting away from you." She looks down at the little clothes she has left. "Not that I want to," I reassure her.

Her mouth drops. "This is how you choose to get away from me? I'm soaked!"

"I had to think fast. I don't trust myself with you." I turn and look at the reflection of my bleeding back. "Take the rest of your clothes off after I leave." Sure, that was a dick thing to do, but I've never had to stop in the middle of something like this. I was desperate.

"Then go." She folds her arms under the running water. "Please Luke. I don't want to see you right now."

"I'll be out of your hair in a second. There are clothes in the closet and food in the kitchen if you get hungry." I scratch the back of my head. "You know what … here," I say, grabbing one of my t-shirts, laying it on the counter. "Oh, and if you need some kind of underwear, I've got boxers and stuff in my top drawer." I point toward my dresser. "Of course, you'll probably have to roll them to keep them up."

"Just go please," she grumbles, without even looking at me.

I nod my head then look over my shoulder. "Is there a time you need to get up?"

"No," she huffs. "Could you just go?"

I hold up my hands. "I'm out. Feel free to sleep in. I'll be on the couch." I give her one last glance then make my over to the door, locking it.

Chapter Eighteen

Reese

My head pounds as I slowly open my eyes and curse at my phone for ringing, snapping out of my coma, when I realize I'm not in my room. The confusion dissipates as pieces of the night before swirl around in my head. *I'm in Luke's bedroom ... Oh my Gosh! I'm in Luke's bedroom!*

Stunned by my realization, I can only sit and take in my surroundings. My phone is lying next to my hair tie on the small nightstand to my left. I'm wearing a T-shirt, that isn't mine, and my dress, bra, and panties are lying on the bathroom floor. I pull down the sheet to find that I am wearing men's boxer briefs, and the mortification immediately sets in.

I jump off the bed and examine the familiar shirt lying on the floor. Gasping when I pick it up, I find it's completely torn and ruined. *He was wearing this. Oh shit! I wasn't dreaming ... I sexually assaulted him!* In a panic, I reach for my phone and pray to God that Gia answers.

"Hello," she says in a chipper tone.

"Thank goodness you answered," I whisper into the phone, squeezing my eyes shut and rubbing my aching temple with my fingers.

"What's wrong, and why are you whispering?"

I look across the room at Luke's bedroom door, hoping he won't hear me. "Everything's wrong. I woke up this morning in Luke's bed!"

"No ... you didn't!"

"I did," I say, nodding, even though she can't see me.

"Did you sleep with him?" she asks, emphasizing the word *sleep*.

I throw my head in my hands as I start to remember details. "Good God, Gia, I'm such a slut."

"Oh my God, you had sex with him? Wait a minute ... were you drunk? Did he take advantage of you? Cuz if he did, then I wi—"

I shake my head, trying to remember the details. "No we didn't have sex, and he didn't take advantage of me," I interrupt. "It's the other way around. I'm trying to remember everything, but it's all choppy."

"What do you mean the other way around?" she asks, and I bite my lip not wanting to tell her. "You're saying you took advantage of him?"

"That's exactly what I'm saying," I growl. Images of the night before continue to form in my mind. "It's all starting to come back." My eyes widen. "Oh my gosh, I'm never drinking again. I remember."

"Do tell, Reese. The suspense is driving me nuts," she quips, and I can hear the smile in her voice.

I look down at the mess on the floor. "He was comforting me, and I took off my dress, asking him to make love to me. All of the sudden I'm forcing him to kiss me, and literally ripping off his shirt. The next thing I remember is I'm in the shower, in my bra and panties, and I'm pissed because he won't have me."

She pauses for a minute, and I check the phone to see if I dropped the call. "You're joking right?" she finally asks.

I hit my aching forehead with the palm of my hand. "I wish I were."

She giggles. "You mean to tell me that you were nearly naked, begged Luke for sex, and he denied you?"

I pull the phone away from my ear and stare at it before saying, "Don't sound too excited. I still have to face him today."

"Huh." She pauses. "I'm impressed."

"Well, I'm humiliated," I grumble, rubbing the spot between my eyes.

"Come on Reese. The only reason he wouldn't sleep with you is because he respects you." She sighs into the phone. "He's not going to let your first time be while you're intoxicated!"

"He doesn't know I'm a virgin." Bunching my eyebrows together, I say, "At least I don't think he knows."

"I can't believe you're in his bedroom right now," she responds, sounding amused.

"Me neither." I chew on my lip. "By any chance can you come get me? I need to get out of here."

"All right, give me directions, and I'm on my way."

I look around the room. "I don't quite remember how we got here." I roll my eyes. "I'll ask him, and then text you the info in a few minutes."

"Okay."

"Thank you," I say, relieved.

"No problem."

I run my fingers through my hair, trying to brush out the tangles. "By the way, have I told you that I'm never drinking again?"

"I can't wait to hear how the rest of the morning goes," she giggles.

"Please, just come get me as soon as I send you directions."

"Okay, good luck!"

"Thanks. I need it."

I grab my hair tie and run to the bathroom to look at my reflection in the mirror. My hair is wild, and my eyes red and puffy. I'm instantly reminded of last night when Luke held me while I sobbed and pleaded in his arms. *No wonder he treats me like a child!* Embarrassment washes over me, and I pray that Luke doesn't walk in. Throwing my hair up quickly, I splash water on my face, and squirt some toothpaste on my finger, before running it back and forth across my teeth. I look at myself one more time and decide there's not much more I can do. I pretty much lost all of my dignity when I begged Luke for a good time last night.

When I try to open the bedroom door, I realize that it's locked from the inside. *Great! I even locked him out of his own room.* I unlock the latch and head down the long narrow hall toward the smell of pancakes, bacon, and something else I can't name. I quietly turn the corner and find Luke placing a pitcher of what looks to be orange juice on the kitchen table. I stand frozen and admire the sight of him. Standing barefoot with his back to me, he is shirtless and there are fresh scratches down his back. My cheeks heat when my eyes zero in, wondering if I am the one to put them there. His faded jeans hang low on his hips, and his hair is a complete mess. My heart speeds up, and I clear my throat to get his attention.

"Morning," he says, glancing at me quickly then turning his gaze to the table.

I'm caught off guard by his nervous reaction. It's not something I've ever seen from him before. "I'm sorry I locked you out of your room, and for the record, I'm never drinking again."

"You didn't lock me out," he says, his voice clipped as I watch him fill a glass. "Orange juice?" he offers.

"Sure, thank you." I press my lips together, giving a small smile. "The door was locked this morning."

"I locked it."

"Why?"

He grips the back of his neck, dropping his gaze to the floor. "To protect you."

I arch a brow and look around the room. "I'm confused, protect me from what? I thought you lived alone?"

He scratches his head, and a partial grin reaches his lips; he's still not looking at me. "I do."

That's when I realize what he means. *He was protecting me from himself. Oh my God, I really am a slut!*

After a few moments of uncomfortable silence he hands me a plate. "I remember you mentioning pancakes before so I thought I'd whip some up. Help yourself. There's some bacon and hash browns over there." He points to the large kitchen island looking dreamy with that tousled hair of his.

"Thank you. It smells great!" I smile, but the small smirk he returns doesn't reach his eyes. "No really, Luke. Thank you ... for everything." I close my eyes, sighing before reopening them. "I'm humiliated by my actions last night." I pause, biting my lip. "I'm not even sure if I remember all that happened, but I know that you tried to fight me off. I've never done something like that before. I'm mortified, and I'm really sorry." I finally lift my gaze to his and am surprised to see understanding in his eyes.

"You had a lot to drink. It happens." His big golden eyes are nothing but sincere. "And that's stretching it a bit when you say I fought it." He clears his throat.

I wait for him to finish, but he doesn't elaborate. Shrugging my shoulders, I add, "Well I don't blame you if you hate me after this."

"You really think I'd hate you?" He sets his fork on his plate then takes a sip of his orange juice with his eyes fixed on mine. "You said you don't know if you remember everything?"

"If you're talking about what happened in your bedroom, please don't make me say it." My cheeks heat as the images replay in my head.

"We need to talk about it."

"Fine," I breathe out. "I remember you and I were talking, and I was emotional. All of the sudden I'm taking off my dress, ripping

154

off your shirt, and oh God …" I cringe. "Begging you to make love to me." I cover my face, searching my brain for the rest before continuing. "Oh, and I forced you to kiss me, leading you to pick me up and put me in the shower, thankfully not naked," I say behind my hands.

"I'm sorry I did that," he says as I peek at him through my fingers. "But I'm not going to say I didn't enjoy it a little." A devilish smirk appears, and his eyes sparkle at me.

"You're sorry?" I point a finger at myself. "I sexually assaulted you, and you're sorry?"

Choking on his orange juice, he clears his throat and says, "You didn't assault me." His eyes look everywhere but in my direction.

"Oh, I think I did."

"Trust me. You didn't."

My mouth drops. "Have you looked in your bedroom lately? I kissed you! I tore the shirt off your back!" I point toward the hall. "There are buttons all over the floor in there."

Dropping his fork a little harder this time, his eyes burn into mine. "I kissed you back Reese, and I didn't want to stop." He slowly shakes his head back and forth. "I almost didn't stop. You have an excuse, what's mine?"

I stare deep into those penetrating eyes, completely surprised by his words. Of course the time that he actually wants to kiss me, I can't even remember it enough to experience what it feels like. Finally I clear my throat and take a sip of orange juice before I speak. "Is that why you locked your door?"

He cocks an eyebrow.

"You lost control … or you were afraid you would?"

There was tension in his gaze as if he didn't want to answer. Then he slowly nods his head, this time not looking away.

"But you did stop," I say softly. Isn't that all that matters?"

He silently stares without saying a word, then runs a hand through his hair before getting up and walking down the hall toward his bedroom. My mind drifts to a pretty blonde female I've been trying hard to forget about. Could *she* be the reason for his behavior? Disappointment courses through me when he comes out moments later wearing a light blue t-shirt. I was enjoying the view of him shirtless and am intrigued by his tattoos. Either way, he's so pretty it hurts, regardless if he's wearing clothes.

I jump when my phone beeps with a text from Gia. "Oh, I uh, need directions to your place. Gia offered to pick me up." I don't know why I feel uncomfortable asking him this.

He sticks his hands in his pockets, rocking back and forth on his feet. "Yeah sure," he says, then gives me what I need, and I text it all back to her.

Feeling a little awkward after our brief exchange, I start clearing the table in an attempt to keep myself busy. "You don't need to do this," he grumbles.

"It's the least I can do."

He chuckles under his breath and follows me to the kitchen.

"What's so funny?" I turn to face him, and he's leaning against the counter, his evil grin back in place, as if last night never happened. I watch his golden eyes sparkle as he gives me a once over, nodding his head appreciatively. "What I would give to know what you're thinking."

"I was just appreciating your," he clears his throat, "underwear."

My face heats as I look down at the white boxer briefs I borrowed. I have them rolled at the waist because I couldn't get them to stay up. "My clothes are still wet. My ... umm ... undergarments included."

"I've never had a woman wear my underwear before."

Holy moly! He finally just called me a woman, and I must say, it feels good. "Sorry." I give a shy smile.

He shrugs his shoulders. "Don't be." My face heats at the way his eyes are watching me.

"Do you mind if I take them home? I'd like to wash them before I give them back. Also, do you have a plastic bag I can put my wet clothes in?"

"Yeah, of course." He runs a hand through his hair, furrowing his brows before looking up to meet my eyes. "Reese, there's something I need to say."

I arch a brow, worried by the look on his face. "Okay."

"You told me something last night and ..." He clenches his jaw like he's having a hard time getting out the words. "Sometimes when we drink, we say things we don't mean." Pinching the bridge of his nose, he continues, "But what you said, I couldn't stop thinking about it—all night and now all morning."

I take out my ponytail and run my fingers through my hair. "You're starting to scare me a little, but go ahead. Ask." He steps closer so that we're standing only a foot apart; he lifts my chin and looks in my eyes.

"What happened between us last night," he says softly. "It can't happen again."

I stare back and swallow the biggest lump I have ever had to swallow. I'm mortified, turned on, relieved, angry, and to be honest, a little hurt. No words could explain the feelings I am experiencing at this point. Thank God for the relief that came when I heard a knock at the door.

Chapter Nineteen

"He said what?" Gia asks, eyes wide.

Covering my face in embarrassment, I tell her, "He said it could never happen again, as if he was worried about me getting the wrong idea."

"And your response was just to stare at him?"

"Yes. You came to my rescue before I could reply. What do I do? What the heck do I tell him?" I mess around with the air vents in her car, needing to feel cold air on my face.

"What was his mood like when he said it?"

I think about the look on his face before he finally had the nerve to tell me. "Sort of ... conflicted, I guess."

She frowns, staring straight ahead. "The man likes you," she says quite certainly. "You'd have to be a dummy not to notice that."

"Well, I'm done playing games." I pick a piece of lint off Luke's shirt. "I think I've put myself out there enough."

Monday morning I made sure to dress in my old clothes. Luke had texted me a couple times, but I couldn't bring myself to respond. I decided on an old pair of gray sweats and a large black t-shirt, not bothering to fix my hair or put on any make-up. What Luke saw the other night was influenced by alcohol—nothing else. Though the feelings I have for him are very much a real thing, I definitely don't want to appear desperate. I'm still without a car so I'm a little nervous about today. The butterflies become more intense when I see him pulling up in his Chevy.

"Thanks for bringing your truck." I shut the door quietly after getting in. "Don't get me wrong, I like the Harley," I say, trying to fill the silence. "I'm just not feeling it today." Finally looking in his direction, I catch him watching me.

"Yeah, sure." He stretches his neck to the left and then the right. "Is everything okay?" he asks, scanning my face, making me fidget in my seat a little. "You never responded to my texts."

"Yeah, everything's fine!" I answer, sounding a little too chipper. "Sorry I didn't respond. I just got really busy." I wasn't going to tell him it took all the willpower I could manage not to respond.

He waits for me to finish.

"I had to do laundry, then I wasn't feeling very well." I try my best to sound natural even though I feel like he can see right through me.

Slowly nodding, he says, "So you decided on comfy today, huh?" His eyes scan me from head to toe.

"Yeah, I figured, why not?"

"Good." He flashes a wide grin. "It suits you."

I hate him.

Narrowing my gaze, I ask, "And why is that, Luke?"

"You know what," he pauses, "forget I said anything."

"No, I'd really like to hear what you have to say."

"Did you get your A/C fixed?" he replies, purposely changing the subject.

I decide to let it go because I just don't feel like arguing with him today. "They finally called me back and said they couldn't get anyone over 'til Thursday. I'm so ready to move."

He taps the steering wheel. "When is your lease up?"

"I still have two months left."

"Have you signed a lease anywhere else?"

I turn to face him. "No, why?"

He purses his lips for a moment then says, "Why don't you break your lease and just stay with me until we find you another place? I'll sleep on my couch." He shrugs. "You can have my bed."

I blink my eyes twice. "You mean like ... move in with you?"

He nods, confusing the hell out of me.

"Do you really think that's a good idea?" I mean yeah, I'm miserable in my apartment, but Luke made it clear that we need to keep some distance. Now he's offering up his place?

"Well yeah. Why wouldn't it be?" He tilts his head to the side, watching me like he can't figure me out.

I look at him blankly because I don't know how to answer that. Finally I say, "How about we start small, and I stay with you until everything is fixed. Maybe I'll find a new place in the process." I can't believe I just agreed to this.

A wry smirk stretches his face. "I'll bring you back tonight to get your clothes, that is, if you don't have any plans?"

"No, I don't have any plans." Seriously? I never have plans.

Glancing at me from the corner of his eyes, he says, "Good."

I can't help but smile, and I don't care if he sees.

"So when are we going to finish our conversation?" Luke asks. He's wearing loose-fitting cotton pants and a white t-shirt I want him to take off.

"What conversation?" I reply, silently praying it has nothing to do with the other night. Ever since that morning I feel awkward whenever he's near. So I straighten my shirt and twiddle my fingers to keep busy while sitting on his couch.

"Why are you nervous?" He tilts his head to the side. "What's wrong?"

Ugh ... why does he notice everything? "Nothing." I tuck my hair behind my ear, trying my best to act normal.

"What conversation are you talking about?"

He watches me suspiciously. "Are you sure nothing's wrong?"

"Yes, I'm sure. Luke, the other night I was drunk and emotional. Tonight … I'm not. So don't worry, there won't be any crying." I wave my hand in a gesture. "Please, continue."

He takes a seat next to me then kicks his feet up on the table, stretching his tattooed arms behind him.

"Comfortable?"

"I am." Turning toward me, he drops his gaze to my shorts, slowly lifting his lashes, and his mouth tilts in a grin. "I like your jammies." He reaches over and tugs on the hem. They're white with little red cherries.

"Thank you," I say, meeting his eyes, wondering why he always touches my clothes.

"You're welcome," he replies, his gaze never wavering.

What is up with him? God, this man is so confusing. "Well?" I arch a brow, waiting.

"Well what?"

I suck in a breath. "You were saying …"

"Oh right, that," he hesitates, and I try my best to be patient. "I wanted to continue our conversation." Looking at me out of the corner of his eyes, he continues, "About the past. About our past, actually." This was something I wasn't expecting, so it took a few seconds to register. "You remember telling me, don't you?"

I do, but I kind of got used to pretending we didn't have one. After what seems like forever, I finally answer his question. "Yes." I curl my legs underneath me. "I remember."

"You know that time when I found you bleeding? When your father was still living there?"

I think about the first time he came to my window. My father was drunk and pushing me around. "You mean the first time we officially met?"

"Yeah, you were holding your little bat, getting ready to take a swing at me." He grins. "My father was like that all the time, with or without alcohol, drugs, or whatever."

This is the first time he's ever brought up his family. The thought of his father hurting him breaks my heart. "I'm sorry." I lay my hand on his shoulder.

He shakes his head. "I'm not telling you to get your sympathy. I'm telling you this because sometimes alcohol changes people. It makes them something they're not."

I raise my eyebrows, encouraging him to continue. "I understand, but you said your father is this way with or without it."

"I'm not talking about my father right now. People can do things when they drink that they might forever regret when they're sober."

I furrow my brows. "Okay, and you're telling me this because?"

"Because some people have remorse for their actions … others don't."

I don't know where he's going with this, but I nod my head. "Yes, I think we gathered that the other night. Get to the point, Luke. What are you trying to say?" I scoot sideways on the couch and again fold my legs underneath me so I'm facing him.

Fixing his eyes on the floor, he purses his lips before he replies, "I think you should talk to your father."

Now *that* catches me by surprise. My mouth drops as I stare at his sincere face for what seems like minutes before responding, "You what?"

"I saw him that night. When he came to see you ..." He swallows. "He's not the same man, Reese. I think you should give him a chance."

I'm shocked. Literally speechless, because I have no idea why he would care about this subject. "You do, huh?" An uncontrollable laugh escapes me. "Oh, this is funny."

"Damn it! It's not funny. It's serious," he growls.

"Thanks for the advice, but I think I've got it figured out." I shake my head. "How could you possibly care about him anyway? You saw how he was."

"Exactly. *Was.*" He leans forward, placing his elbows on his knees. "I think some people deserve second chances, that's all. You know I care about you." He watches me carefully, and I nod my head in response. I do believe he cares about me. If I'm being honest, I think about my father all the time. I'm just not sure what to do about the situation, or if I'll ever be ready to talk with him.

"Look, all I ask is that you'll think about it. All right?" He tucks a strand of hair behind my ear. "Can you do that for me?" His voice is soft.

I don't know why I give him what he wants, but I'm unable to argue any longer. "Okay," I murmur. "I'll think about it."

The corner of his mouth tips, and he nudges me with his shoulder. "Come here," he says, pulling me in for an intoxicating hug. "Thank you."

Enjoying this new side of him, I shut my eyes and squeeze him tighter, hoping we can do this more often. "Luke," my voice is muffled with my face pressed into his chest.

"Hmm?"

"Is this off limits?"

"Is what?"

I shiver as his breath blows against the crook of my neck. "You and I hugging, is it off limits?"

"Hell no," he grumbles. When I pull away, he flashes his dimples.

"Good, cuz you smell amazing."

He tilts his head to the side. "I do?"

"Like a breath of fresh air." I grin.

Slowly eyeing me up and down, he says, "Yeah, well, so do you." Then he gets off the couch and walks toward the kitchen. "You thirsty?" He grabs a couple waters from the fridge before I can answer. "Come on, I want to show you something." He hands me a bottle then pulls a blue blanket out of the closet.

Chapter Twenty

Reese

I stop and stare at the black and white photos on the wall. Several are from his fights—one where he's raising his hand in a fist, another where he's wearing a huge gold belt around his waist, smiling. He's shirtless and a little bloody in both, but still looks as handsome as ever. I don't think it's possible for him not to. "Do you miss it?" I ask, noticing him leaning against the wall behind me.

"I miss the fights." He shrugs his shoulders. "Not the fame or the lifestyle."

"What about the women?" I grin.

"I'm done with that, too." Stepping closer, he gives my heart a little jolt. God, this man sends mixed signals. "I'd say they go with the lifestyle." He presses his lips into a tight line. "Come on."

I put on my flip-flops then follow him outside. We climb a winding staircase leading up to the rooftop. "Wow." I look around, admiring the perfect little set up. There's a table with two chairs and a hammock that's cemented in place. There's even a few potted plants scattered around in various spots, and they all look like they've been taken care of. "I never knew this was up here." I watch him lay down the blanket, feeling the cool night air on my skin. "Do you come up here a lot?"

"At night when it's cool." He lies back against the blanket, resting his head in his hands. "There's nothing like a star-filled Arizona sky." I walk over toward the blanket and sit in the spot where he pats beside him. "Sometimes I come up here to think ... clear my head."

I lay back, taking the same position, looking up at the countless number of stars above. "It's beautiful." I stare in amazement. "I'm jealous you have this. It's just so," I pause, looking for the words. "So peaceful."

He doesn't say anything for a minute. I figure it's because he's enjoying the silence. After lying there for a while he says, "Your lease is up in December, right?"

I turn to face him. "Yeah, why?"

"The place next door ..." He looks at me. "I own it."

"You do?"

He nods his head. "My tenants are moving out next month. It's an exact replica of this one—two bedrooms, two bathrooms, a patio on the roof—there's plenty of room. It'd be perfect for you."

I look away, facing the stars again. "That's extremely kind of you to offer, but I don't have the kind of money for something like this, and I can't imagine having you as my landlord." I give him a sideways glance. "No offense or anything."

"None taken." I hear the smile in his voice before he adds, "What if I don't want your money?"

"Then I'll take it!" I laugh.

"I'm serious." Judging by his tone, he is serious.

I look at him pointedly. "What do you mean?" *Because obviously I'm not quite understanding.*

"I mean, what if I give it to you?"

I look at him like he's crazy. Because … well, because he is. "Sorry, it's just that, I don't think I understand what you're saying." I sit up, leaning back on my elbows. "You would give me the condo next door, in exchange for nothing?"

"Absolutely." He grins. "I own it free and clear. I own the complex."

I blink a couple times. "All of these?" Not that there are a lot of them, but I'm just surprised.

He nods.

"How many are there?" I remember Pam telling me he invested his money in property, but I didn't ask her to elaborate on the topic.

"Five."

"That must have been expensive. These are nice. I mean *really* nice."

"I had the money to do it and figured if I invested in property, my rentals would supply a good income."

I smile. "That's smart, Luke. I'm impressed."

He turns away and gazes straight up to the sky. It feels different lying out here next to him—like something has shifted between us. He reaches out and twirls a loose strand of my hair around his finger. "So, what do you say?"

I shut my eyes and let out a shaky breath. "Why would you do this for me? I mean, God Luke! You confuse the hell out of me!" I bite my lip, eyeing him down while he rubs the new whiskers growing on his chin. He looks devastatingly sexy. I can barely stand it.

"For several reasons." He pauses. "None of them I feel like mentioning." He slowly turns his gaze to mine then softly chuckles when my mouth drops.

"Well, that's fine. You don't have to give me a reason, because I can't accept your offer." As tempting as it is, there's just no way. *I mean, really ... a free condo?* "Thank you though."

"You'll change you're mind." He grins wickedly. "I knew you would say that, by the way."

I stare into his warm brown eyes before dropping my gaze to those perfectly sculpted lips. I mean, let's be real here. I'm twenty years old, and the only lip action I've gotten was when I was too hammered to remember the details.

"What are you thinking?" he asks, his eyes following the same pattern as mine.

"About Lauren." My cheeks feel hot. Yes, she was in the back of my mind, but no, I wasn't planning on bringing her up ... at least not yet.

His brows bunch together. "What about Lauren?"

Trying to figure out exactly how to word, but finally giving up, I say, "Shouldn't you offer the place to her? Wouldn't she be a little offended?"

He cocks an eyebrow, and I continue to ramble as he watches me. "With you offering the place to someone other than her? A *woman* for that matter!"

He sits up, scanning my face. "She might be if I didn't already take care of that issue for her. And she seems pretty happy with what she's got."

My heart sinks, and I take the rubber band off my arm, throwing my hair up, in order to distract myself. "Does she know I'm staying with you?"

"No." He reaches over and gently pulls the band out of my hair. "Leave it down."

I try my best to ignore what just happened, and from the look on his face, I'm guessing he is, too.

Lying back down, he fixes his eyes on the stars and asks, "Why would I need to tell Lauren you're here?"

For some reason his question strikes a nerve. I may not know much about relationships, but I'm not stupid. "Hmm, let's see. Maybe because when you're in a relationship with someone, it's important to be honest with that person?" Narrowing my eyes, I ask, "Haven't you ever heard of that before?"

He cocks a brow. "You're accusing me of being dishonest?"

I hold out my hand. "Please, let me finish."

The corner of his mouth tips, making me want to punch him. *Is he really laughing at me right now?*

"For someone as noble as yourself, you seem to be pretty clueless when it comes to women." I lie back down, crossing my arms awkwardly, then turn and gaze at the stars. "And feelings!"

"Oh really?" He chuckles playfully, but I don't find it very funny.

"Yes really," I growl back.

Before I can blink, my wrists are pinned above my head, and Luke is lying on top of me. "What ..." I try to speak, breathless, with my heart hammering hard in my chest. "What are you doing?"

He secures his body over mine so that our faces are close. "I'm going to make you listen." A devilish grin stretches his face. My insides tingle in several different places. "And there isn't anything you can do about it." He slowly lifts his lashes, and those eyes pierce into mine. "I've been meaning to tell you." He leans down and presses his lips against my skin, inhaling the space behind my ear. "Lauren isn't my girlfriend." He breathes, bringing goose bumps all over my flesh. "She's my sister."

"She's what?" I ask, panting. If he just said what I think he said, then I need to hear it again.

He lifts his head to look at my face. "You heard me."

"Why would you do that?" I ask, surprised. "You knew I thought she was your girlfriend."

He pulls a hair out of my face. "At first I was going to tease you about it—mess with you a bit. I planned on eventually telling you, but ... then I figured it was for the best."

"For the best?" I arch a brow, confused. "And now?"

"Now I don't know what to think." He rolls off me, looking toward the sky.

"If it's for the best, then why did you tell me?"

"My life ..." he pauses. "It's complicated. I didn't want to subject you to it. You're worth more than that."

"And now?"

"I still don't," he says, watching me carefully. "But I'm not sure how much longer I can stay away." His gaze falls to my lips then back to my eyes. "I'm trying. Honestly, I am."

Chapter Twenty-One

"There's still a lot about you that I don't know." We stayed beneath the stars for about an hour. Now, we're stretched out on his bed with our backs against the headboard, stuffed after sharing a pizza.

The corner of his mouth turns up. "What do you want to know?"

"Everything."

He takes a deep breath then lets it all out. "I don't have a favorite color, probably because I'm colorblind."

I arch an eyebrow, interrupting. "You're colorblind?"

"Yeah." He shrugs.

"Hmm." I nod my head, thinking about his wardrobe selection—the mostly white, black, or gray t-shirts I usually see him in, then realize he's waiting for me to give him the go ahead. "Sorry. Go on. What kind of music do you like?"

He chuckles. "All types, but I have a few favorites."

"Give me two of your favorite bands?"

"One of them is a given—Linkin Park," he says pointedly, and I smile back, letting him know I agree. "They help me focus. I take it you agree."

"I do. In fact, they're also one of my favorites."

He scratches his head. "Yeah, they have a pretty big fan base I guess. Fort Minor is another good one. It all depends on my mood ... or where I am."

"So you like the harder stuff?"

He cocks a brow, looking distracted. "What's that?"

"You mainly listen to the heavy stuff?"

"When I'm training, but when I just want to chill I could go for pretty much anything."

"Who's another one of your favorites?"

He crosses his arms, looking up at the ceiling. "Coldplay."

I get up on my knees, excited. "No way!"

His eyes sparkle as he tilts his head to the side. "Yes way."

"Do you have any idea how much I love them?" I ask, bouncing up and down like a twenty-year old child. He shakes his head back and forth, clearly amused by my enthusiasm.

"I have been dying to see them in concert." I grab his shoulders. "Every time they go on tour, something comes up, where I can't afford the ticket. Did you know they're performing here next month?" I say excitedly, placing my hands flat against his chest. There's a shift in his eyes, and I'm suddenly aware of his fingers digging into my hips. My face heats when I realize, that I'm straddling him. "Oh my God," I breathe.

The corner of his mouth tilts in a slow, sexy grin, before his teeth gently bite down on his lip, and he grips me tighter.

The heat in his eyes makes my heart pound like crazy, and I can barely find my voice. "I'm sorry," I say, slowly climbing off of him. The smirk is back in place when his gaze drops to his pants.

"Yeah, me too." He laughs. My eyes follow, and I gulp at the huge tent that wasn't there a minute ago. "I'm gonna need a cold shower," he says.

Feeling awkward during the silence, I ask, "Does it help?"

He cocks a brow.

"I mean with …" I point at his obvious erection.

"Yes, it helps." He nudges me with his shoulder. "I'm not going to make you say it." My face reddens, embarrassed that I can't say, "penis" or "erection" in front of him. He grabs a pillow and places it over his pants, and I quickly think of something to change the subject.

"What are your biggest fears?"

Laughing at my nervousness, he says, "My turn." He reaches over and squeezes my thigh. "We'll get back to me later."

"Fine." I shrug. "I have nothing to hide."

He lays his head back against the headboard then turns his face toward mine, eyeing me playfully. "The other night when you attacked me …" He smirks.

"Don't even start, Ryann!" I elbow him in his side. "Believe me, it only happened because of the alcohol," I lie. Gia's always tells me I'm a terrible liar so I make sure not to look him in the eye.

"I was teasing," he says softly. "I like seeing you all riled up. But what I have to say, does have to do with the other night."

"Go on then." I gesture with my hands, figuring he might as well lay it out there.

Scratching his chin as he watches me carefully, he asks, "Do you remember telling me you're a virgin?"

I throw my head in my hands. "Do we really have to talk about this?" I mean come on! I get to learn about favorite colors and music, and he gets right to the virginity question? WTF?

"So it's true?"

"Not that it's any of your business, but yes. I am very much a virgin."

He removes my hands from my face and asks, "And you're ashamed of this because?"

"I'm not ashamed that I'm a virgin. I'm ashamed of my behavior the other night," I sigh. "It's a little embarrassing, that's all." He looks at me like he's debating asking me more. "Go ahead. Tell me what you're thinking."

He pauses then asks, "Has anyone ever touched you?" He hesitates, "I don't know everything that went down that day with Ronald, but I'm not talking about him, and it's not my business. What I mean is, has anyone ever touched you ... when you wanted it?"

The mention of Ronald sort of ruined the moment for me, and I can't believe he's asking me this. But the truth is, because of Luke, Ronald didn't touch me, and I'll forever be grateful to him for it. As far as anyone after, I had no desire for that kind of intimacy, at least not until now. "Ugh, aren't you supposed to be asking about my favorite color or what kind of movies I like?" I whine. "This is seriously humiliating."

"I guess I find your virginity a lot more interesting, and you said you had nothing to hide." He leans over and lightly tugs on my hair. "You don't have to answer if it makes you uncomfortable."

"No, you're right." I nod. "I told you I had nothing to hide so I'm just going to come out and say it. It's just hard to say the words out loud." I look down at the duvet, making circles over the pattern with my fingers. The quiet makes me afraid to see his reaction once I answer. "I've never had a boyfriend or wanted any of the touching stuff you're talking about. Are you happy now?" I lift my eyes to meet his, all humor washed away. There's no way I'm going to tell him he was my first kiss.

"Wow," is all he says.

"Yeah, wow," I say back, then tuck a strand of hair behind my ear.

"You're smart, you're funny, you're confident, beautiful inside out, but you've never been touched. How is that even possible?" he asks, watching me carefully.

My heart rate picks up. "I've never given anyone a chance."

"So that's why you have a hard time saying penis?" A grin slides across his face then he holds up the pillow that was covering his lap, ready to block me.

My cheeks heat. "You know what, Luke, your turn is officially over!"

"What?" His brows lift. "It's cute."

"Yeah, I bet."

"I swear it." He runs a hand through his hair then climbs off the bed, surprising me. "I should take a shower." I can't help but stare as he takes off his shirt then quickly balls it up in his hands. "Can I get you anything?"

I blink twice; entranced by his ripped chest, I then drop my eyes to his perfectly sculpted abs. "I'm good."

His eyebrows bunch together for a second. "I guess I'll see you in the morning then. Goodnight." He flashes me a half grin then turns around and walks toward the door.

My heart feels heavy. I don't want him to leave. "Luke," I call out, and he glances over his shoulder. "You can sleep in here." I pat the spot next to me, still warm from where he left it. "I promise I won't take off my clothes." I frown at my own words the moment they leave my mouth.

His eyes twinkle. "What about mine?"

"Those are safe, too."

He stretches his arms at his sides, gripping the doorframe. "I've never slept with a woman in my bed before." Cocking a brow, he continues, "And I've never slept with a virgin." He chuckles. "Never mind."

"I trust you," I say softly.

"You shouldn't."

"Well I do."

He throws his shirt over his shoulder and slowly walks away from me. "All right then, I'll see you in a few. Get ready to cuddle." I watch him go with a huge smile on my face.

Chapter Twenty-Two

Reese

A few days of staying with Luke turned out to be a month. Although I finally got my car back, a maintenance man from the apartment complex called and told me it would take two weeks to get the new part they ordered before they could fix my air conditioner. They offered to put me up in a hotel, but Luke insisted I stay with him instead. Every time I look into those eyes I have a hard time saying no. Which brings me to my future living arrangements.

Gia is really good at convincing me to do things I normally wouldn't do. Not that they're bad things—she just likes to take more risks, and I've always envied that about her. When I explained to Luke that I hadn't told her about the condo, he decided to take matters into his own hands and tell her himself.

"Are you crazy!" she yelled. "He offered you a condo, and you said no!" We were sitting in class as several students turned in our direction.

"Would you keep it down?" I growl then glare at Luke, who's openly grinning next to me.

The conversation went on for days until Gia finally convinced me of all the fun we would have as roommates: decorating together, watching chick flicks, and of course, tormenting our handsome neighbor. That was two weeks ago, and every day since, Luke and I've been working, living, and sleeping together. And when I say sleeping, I mean sleeping. Not once has he tried to touch or kiss me, although the tension between us is hard to ignore. Sometimes I think I'm imagining it, wondering if I'm the only one that feels it. An accidental brush of our bodies, a lingering gaze, or the times when he tightens his jaw as if he's about to say something, but stops himself, or even worse—walks away, leaving me confused. Why does he hold back? I'm tired of him holding back.

I've been lying awake for the past ten minutes, but haven't moved an inch. The upper part of my body is pressed against Luke's hard chest. My left arm is wrapped around his waist. I think I might have even drooled a little, but what surprises me more is the large tan hand that's resting securely on my butt. I have no recollection of how we got in this position, but I'm afraid if I move, I'll wake him. The feel of his taught skin as he unknowingly holds me close is something I'd like to savor.

The first night when he said we would cuddle, I fell asleep before he hopped back in bed. When I woke up a few hours later, I found him lying as far from me as possible. In fact, I'm surprised I didn't find him on the floor. But every single night he's been inching his way closer, and I stay in place, protecting my ego and my pride.

My cell phone rings violently on the nightstand beside me. His fingers grip my ass before a soft snore escapes him. Letting out a quiet chuckle, I take a long hard look at his face. God, I want to kiss those lips, that mouth, his dimples …

"Don't Reese," his gravelly voice mumbles, then he snores again, squeezing my butt even tighter. I bite back a giggle—glad I didn't get caught. *Could he possibly be dreaming about me? And how in the heck can he sleep through this noise?* I watch his lips move.

"Don't beg. Please." His eyebrows furrow together. "I already showed you earlier."

Don't beg? What the hell? I scoot up a little closer, leaning my ear toward his mouth when his grip on my bottom increases.

"I'll flex one more time. That's it."

My mouth drops before a grin slides across his face.

"You faker!" I shout unable to hide the smile.

He opens an eye, chuckling, and I pick up a pillow and whack him with it.

"Are you enjoying yourself?" I look back at his hand.

He fakes innocence. "I woke up, and it was already there; as for afterward, yeah I'm a guy."

My phone rings again, interrupting us, and I press a finger to my mouth, in an attempt to keep him quiet. "Hey Mom."

"I've called you at least ten times. Why aren't you answering your phone?" she asks sternly. It's obvious she's a little pissed.

Just when I'm about to give an excuse, Luke gets out of bed with a huge bulge in his pants, and I fail to pretend I didn't see it. I swear, it's like every morning he has a boner. Is that normal? I have no idea, but I'm definitely not asking him.

"Reese?" my mom's high pitch voice calls in the distance.

"Yeah." I close my mouth, realizing it's still open.

"Are you listening to me?"

"Y-yeah Mom, I heard you." I watch Luke's shirtless body stride toward me, noticing some scars I hadn't seen on him before. He cocks a brow, and my eyes follow as he makes his way to the bathroom. *Good Lord, what is wrong with me?*

I clear my throat. 'Sorry, I couldn't get to it in time. That's all."

"Well, it's a good thing you finally answered. I have some news."

That got my attention. "You and Tim broke up?" I ask, a little too happily.

"Oh no, nothing like that. It's good news, actually. Tim and I are …" she pauses.

"You and Tim are …" I try to move the conversation along before Luke says something in the background and she hears him.

"Tim and I are moving out of state."

My heart sinks, and I fall back, letting my head hit the pillow. "What do you mean out of state? Like far away out of state?"

"Yes!" she squeals.

"How far?"

"Very far. North Carolina far, to be exact."

I'm stunned silent, before I ask, "Why North Carolina?" I'm trying like hell to hold back the sudden rush of tears. "It's on the other side of the country."

"Tim's family is there, and he misses them. We both feel he needs to be closer."

"But he doesn't have any children."

"He has his brother and his mother."

"I see," my voice is clipped.

"See, I knew you would."

"What about the money? How in the world can you to afford it?" It's not like Tim has a bunch of cash lying around, and I know my mom doesn't have any.

"His mother's going to help us. You know, until we get on our feet," she says it as though the problem is solved. "There's no need for you to worry, Reese."

"Uh huh." Easy for you to say, Mom. "So when are you planning on leaving? I mean, how much longer do I have with you?" I wipe away an escaping tear.

"Well … we're leaving in a week." She sighs. "And I'm going to be pretty busy until then, so let's try and pick a time to schedule you in." I pause, closing my eyes for a few seconds, not knowing what to say. "You still there?"

"Yeah Mom. I'm just taking it all in." I look around for Luke, noticing he's nowhere in sight.

"Oh, and I'm going to need you to come get the rest of your stuff anyway, otherwise we'll have to dump it."

"Okay," I say, wiping away the rest of my tears. "Maybe I can come by tomorrow."

"That'll be perfect. Just call before you come."

"I will." I take a deep breath. "I love you."

"Love you too, baby."

I squeeze the phone a little tighter. "Bye."

There's a small knock at the bedroom door. "You okay?" Luke asks, still shirtless. His arms are raised above his head, as he grips the doorframe.

"Yeah." I give a weak smile, although having him here makes me feel better.

"You want to talk about it?"

Not wanting to gawk, my eyes flick to the floor. "That was my mom."

"Yeah, I knew that." He slowly steps closer to the bed. "What did she say?"

"That she's moving across the country to follow her asshole boyfriend."

There's a pause before he asks, "Does he hit her?"

"Who doesn't?"

The bed sinks beside me. "I'm sorry."

I bite hard on my lip, willing myself not to cry. "Who's going to help her? Where's she going to go?" My face falls in my hands. "What if he ..."

"It's not yours to carry," his voice is soothing as he reaches out, pulling me into a warm hug. "She's a grown woman, Reese. You have to let her make her own choices."

"But what if those choices kill her."

"They're still her choices. It's a risk you're going to have to take." He pulls away and wipes the tears off my face. "I don't like seeing you cry."

I'm sure the image he's looking at isn't pretty. My hair is most likely a mess, and I haven't even brushed my teeth yet. "Sorry," I remark. "I'm being a baby, aren't I?"

"I didn't say that. I just don't like seeing you hurt," he answers sincerely.

My eyes rest on the small scar below his bottom lip. Without even thinking, I reach out and run my thumb across it. He doesn't back away or flinch. Instead, he watches me with careful eyes. "How did you get this scar?"

He gives a half smirk then turns away. "A fight."

I can tell this is a touchy subject, but I grab a pillow and settle it into my lap, preparing to ask him more. "In the cage?"

He lies on his back and stares at the ceiling. "In juvie."

I suck in a breath, trying to mask my shock. I don't want him to think I'm judging him. "Why? I mean ... what did you do?"

He glances at me sideways. "Which time?"

"You were there more than once?" Pam told me he had gotten into trouble, but I never imagined, this was the trouble she was talking about.

"I was."

"For what?" My voice squeaks before I toss the pillow behind me.

"Several things—drugs, stealing, fighting ... you name it." His head moves back and forth and his gaze looks far away. "I was a messed up kid, Reese. Still am." Everything in his tone sounds final, and the pain behind it breaks my heart. Sure I'm surprised by his admission, but the boy he used to be is not the man he is now, not even close.

I lie down next to him, hesitant about what to say. "You're not that person anymore. You were young. You're different now."

His eyes fall on mine. "What makes you so sure?"

"Oh, I'm sure." I reach for his hand. "It's your past, Luke. I'm not judging you for it."

His eyes turn back toward the ceiling. "When did this become about me?" he replies. "I thought I was comforting you."

"You are. See? I'm already feeling better." I give him the biggest smile I can muster. "Now, it's your turn ... and I'm curious."

He sighs, clearly not happy with this idea. "What do you want to know?"

Everything, but it's obvious he doesn't like to share. "When was the last time you were arrested?"

"Nine years ago."

"So you were sixteen?"

"I was."

"That was three years before Ro— ... before you saved me." I squeeze his hand, not wanting to speak the name of my attempted rapist unless I have to. "I know I've told you this before, but I can never tell you enough. Thank you. If it wasn't for you that night,

I … I don't know where I'd be today." I swallow the lump in my throat as the memory plays vividly in my head.

His jaw tightens. "I should have gotten there earlier; I should have shot the fucker."

"Stop it Luke. You did the right thing." His eyes move to my face. Anyway, enough about him, tell me about the bad boy you used to be." I wiggle my eyebrows to lighten the mood. "What was the last thing you were arrested for?"

He cocks a brow like I'm insane, but finally says, "Drugs and armed robbery."

"Did you act alone? I mean … someone must have influenced you. Am I right?"

"I make my own choices," he finally says. "I'm responsible for myself."

"So you acted alone?" I watch his Adam's apple bob in his throat as he swallows.

"No."

"Who was with you?"

His head snaps in my direction. "What is this? Twenty questions?"

"I told you, I want to know everything, even the parts you're not proud of. It's not going to make me think less of you."

"My father." He runs a hand through his hair, blowing out a breath. "I was with my father."

His answer catches me off guard. I knew his father wasn't good to him but had no idea it was to this extreme. "Your father?"

Unexpected tears prick the back of my eyes. "Where was your mother?"

"My mother's dead," his voice is clipped, and my heart instantly drops to my stomach. He gives a dry laugh. "She asked me not to go, begged my father to keep me out of it, but I went, and that was the last time I saw her."

I'm speechless. The torment in his eyes is my undoing. "I ... I don't know what to say." Warm tears rush down my cheeks. "I'm so sorry."

"Aw c'mon, Reese. Don't cry." He reaches over and brushes my tears with his thumb.

"It's just that I can tell you blame yourself. It's not your fault." I hiccup. "If anyone is to blame, it's your father."

"See what I went and did?" He tips my chin then raises a brow.

"You didn't do anything."

"Look, can we change the subject? Today's supposed to be a good day. I don't want to ruin it with all this depressing talk."

I nod, even though there's more I want to ask him, like how his mother died, and where was Lauren during all of this?

"Good. You hungry?" He grins, and his face tells me the conversation is over.

"Starving actually."

"Me too." He makes his way over to the door and says, "Get dressed. I've got a place in mind."

Chapter Twenty-Three

Reese

Luke takes me to a bagel shop a couple of blocks away. We both order a plain bagel with cream cheese, and a much needed cup of coffee, before finding a seat on the patio. The weather is exceptionally cool for the middle of October, and we plan to enjoy it for as long as we can.

"You excited about tonight?" he asks, taking the lid off his coffee, while he stirs in a packet of sugar. He's wearing a white baseball cap turned backward, full dimples on display. A look that works well on him, then again everything works well on him.

I arch an eyebrow, not having a clue what he's talking about. "Excited?"

He purses his lips. "Did you forget already?" He takes a bite of his bagel, watching as I search my brain for memory.

Tilting my head to the side, I respond, "I guess I did."

"That hurts."

"What?" I ask, honestly confused.

"I told you there's somewhere I'm taking you tonight." He lightly taps my knee with his. "It's cool though." He shrugs, teasing me.

"I'm sorry." I vaguely remember Luke asking if I had plans, but that's about all my brain will give me. I lean back in my chair, giving him my full attention. "I guess I've been a little distracted." Since the phone call with my mom, and the conversation he and I had earlier, it's all I can think about.

"You don't need to apologize. I get it." The corner of his mouth curves before he softly says, "I've got something that's going to cheer you up." His eyes sparkle as he bites down on his lip. *I think you just did*, I want to tell him. My curiosity is peaked when his smile widens and he says, "You are going to love me," then takes the last bite of his bagel, eyes never leaving mine.

"Okay, you've got my interest. Where are you taking us?" I can't help but smile at the adorable expression on his face.

He crosses his arms over his chest, grinning devilishly. "Wouldn't you like to know?"

I throw my napkin at him before finally finishing off my bagel, then grab our plates, and toss them in the garbage. "Let's go then, Mr. Cocky; I need to shower and get ready." All this talk is getting me excited.

He turns his hat back around, pieces of his hair flipping out the bottom. "You have time. Concert doesn't start 'til seven."

I stop what I'm doing, and look at him pointedly, feeling a rush of adrenaline running through me. "Did you just say concert?" *Please say that I heard him correctly.*

He gives me his amazing half smile as he confidently strides closer. By the look on his face, I'm not sure how much longer I can hold his gaze. Once the tips of our toes touch, he leans down, pressing his lips against my ear, making me shiver. "That's what I said," his silky voice is just above a whisper.

My breathing picks up for two very different reasons. "You're taking me to the Coldplay concert?" I'm surprised I'm even able to speak.

"I am." His eyes swirl with flecks of gold and brown.

A huge grin I can't contain stretches across my face. "You're right." I wrap my arms around him. "I do love you."

The water pressure here is heaven compared to my apartment. Luke took off to the grocery store, so I decided to enjoy the luxuries of one of his fancy showers. I'm in the second bathroom this time, surprised to see that both bathrooms are identical. They come with dual showerheads, are big enough to fit at least five, and even have a little loveseat where I can conveniently shave my legs. The walls and floors are covered in stone, bringing a nice touch to the rest of the modern look. Everything is so … well, nice. I guess it's one of the perks of being a successful cage fighter. It's funny how I never really watched the sport, always dreaming about Luke, wondering how he was, when all I needed to do was flip on the television. Would I have recognized him then? Would things be different between us? Speaking of … ugh, I set down my coconut body wash wondering what time it is? Thinking about our relationship could take days, and frankly, it's exhausting.

After rinsing out the last of the conditioner, I turn off the water and reach for a towel. Except, there is no towel, and I'm dripping all over the floor, looking around the bathroom, when my eyes finally land on the steam-covered mirror. I take a couple steps forward and wipe away some of the fog, gazing at my naked reflection. "Crap!" *Now what am I going to do?* I put my dirty clothes in the wash after Luke left, not even bothering to bring anything with me. *So incredibly stupid!* I bite my lip, rocking back and forth on my heels, listening for any noises outside the bathroom walls. I place my ear against the door before slowly pulling it open. "Hello," I say quietly at first, my heart thundering deep in my chest. "Luke." I make my voice louder, still getting no response. "Thank God." I sigh, covering my intimate parts, carefully tiptoeing down the hall toward the bedroom.

When I hear a noise behind me, I turn and cower, frozen in the middle of the hallway. *What was that?* I walk toward the sound, finding it's coming from my clothes spinning in the washer. Rolling my eyes at my paranoia before turning back around, I slam into what seems to be a person, startling the hell out of me. I jump then everything happens in slow motion. The wood floor makes is hard to keep my balance. "Argh!" I shout, trying to stop myself from falling forward.

"Oomph." I grab on to a hard, naked chest. *Oh my gawd!* Luke's arms wrap around my waist the instant our bodies collide, and now that we've safely landed, he still hasn't let go.

"I'm sorry," I mumble into his skin, slowly lifting my head, finding his brown eyes piercing into mine. His dark hair is coated in droplets of water, and his scent reminds me of soap with a hint of rain. I've never been completely naked in front of anyone. To say I'm mortified would be an understatement. My eyes fall to my naked breast, and I press tighter against him, covering myself.

"Come here," his voice is rough, as he scoots me up, aligning our faces.

The electricity from him touching my skin makes me tremble, and the intensity in his eyes is enough to forget my thoughts. "I was looking for a ..." My attempt to explain my nakedness is seriously lacking. "There was no towel in the ..."

He wraps a hand in my hair then closes his eyes, distracting me. "The way you smell." He brings his nose to the crook of my neck. "Mmm, it drives me crazy." I feel his breath on me as he softly chuckles against my flesh. "I knew you were going to be trouble, but damn why do you do this to me?"

Chills break out on my body. "Why do you do this to me?" I breathe. The man is driving me crazy with the tone of his voice alone.

Carefully running his fingertips up my spine, he whispers, "Your skin is so soft." What feels to be his arousal reminds me of my nakedness. "I can't get you out of my head."

Dropping my gaze, I notice the towel hanging low on his hips. My eyes lift to his as he watches me. "Did you see?" A mental picture of me, naked and cowering in the hall, pops in my head.

The corner of his mouth slowly angles, turning into a full-blown grin as he nods his head. "Ohhh yeahhh."

My cheeks heat, as I swallow down a large lump in my throat. "Will you close your eyes so I can get up?"

His eyes sparkle, and he tucks a strand of hair behind my ear. "I'm not letting you go yet."

My pulse picks up, and I bite my lip nervously. "I can't just lay on top of you naked all day." Okay, that probably wasn't the best thing to say, but the past couple days I've been crazy horny, and when Luke teases me with his words it only makes it worse. Sort of like an all bark no bite kind of thing.

"What are you thinking?" he asks. I have a distinct feeling that he already knows.

"Nothing. It really doesn't matter."

"Why do you say that?"

I feel the tips of his fingers making circles on my back, causing another rash of chills over my skin. I avoid the question, unable to look at him anymore. "We should get ready." I can't be the one always putting my feelings on the line. If he wants me, he needs to be a man about it. These games he plays are confusing as hell.

"Wait." He holds me tighter, clenching his jaw, apparently frustrated. Who with? I'm not sure, but I lie still watching his gaze turn hungry as his eyes fall on my lips. "I want to kiss you." His fingers grip the back of my neck, and he slowly lifts his lashes. "Can I kiss you?" The tenderness in his voice melts my heart into a puddle. I can't even speak or breathe a response, but the look on my face is all he needs.

Bringing his mouth to mine, he hesitates, with a soft peck before gently pulling my bottom lip into his mouth. He gives the top the same attention, brushing his lips back and forth in a sweet caress. When I follow his lead, the kiss turns more eager, and it's not long before I feel the light graze of his tongue. I open to him, and a breathy moan, which I'm unable to hold back, escapes.

In a sudden movement, he flips me over, groaning as he takes full claim over my mouth. He holds himself up on his forearms, his hands placed flat above my head. His knees are spread over me, framing my thighs, and in a husky voice he whispers, "I've been wanting to do this for too long."

His words make me shiver. My heart feels like it's going to explode. If this is what kissing him feels like, I can't imagine the sex. He hasn't even touched me, but every nerve in my body ignites. His open mouth runs along my jaw, then the tip of his tongue drags down my throat. His lips, and the sensation of his minty breath, have me trembling. From head to toe, my skin feels like it's on fire.

"Luke," it comes out as a whimper, as I place my hands over the ripples in his back. The ache to have him touch me is overwhelming, but I don't want to ask him. I'm not going to be weak this time.

Tugging on my lobe with his teeth, he says, "Say it again," before he kisses me gently. We continue like this for a while, as he switches back and forth, holding my face then wrapping my hair in his fingers. When I finally feel like his hands are ready wander, he tenses, and slowly pulls away, meeting my gaze.

I notice an obvious shift in his features as I stare into those pools of amber. Having a good idea of what he's about to tell me, I beat him to it. My pride deserves a break. "We need to stop," I say, clearing my throat.

He eyes me carefully and rolls off, standing and securing his towel. "You're right," he replies, making his way over to the bathroom.

I pull my knees up, wrapping my arms around them, feeling more embarrassed than before. "What was I thinking?" I tuck my hair behind my ear, hoping I sound convincing. "I shouldn't have let you," I say, reminding him it was his idea.

He walks back, holding a shirt and towel, pursing his lips as he drops them down beside me. "It's not your fault," he says, running a hand through his hair. "You didn't do anything."

I pull his shirt over my head, and he looks away. "I guess I'll um ..."

"I shouldn't have disrespected you like that," he interrupts. I look over my shoulder to find him intensely watching me.

"Seeing you ..." He points toward the hall. "Naked ..." He drops his gaze down my body, and taking his time to bring it back up, he squeezes his eyes shut. "And wet ..." He sighs, rubbing the space between his brows. "I had a moment of weakness ... you deserve to be respected."

His stare makes me feel all warm inside, but I don't know how to respond to what he just said, so I reply, "You do respect me. You always have."

He leans down, placing a gentle kiss against my forehead. His mouth lingers a bit before he pulls away and mumbles, "You're breaking me Reese. Stop now if you know what's good for you."

"Stop what?" I pause. "I don't even know what I'm doing."

Two dimples frame his perfect mouth. "I guess that makes two of us."

Chapter Twenty-Four

Reese

The look on Luke's face when I walked out of his room made the ache in my feet well worth it—not to mention I came prepared, bringing my cutest pair of flats, assuming I would need them at some point tonight. I chose to wear a little white tank and a light blue jean skirt. The skirt is super short. Not to the point that my butt is hanging out, but my three-inch red heels are definitely garnering attention. Luke's seems to be battling keeping his hands off me. It's a side of him I'm not used to seeing. It makes me smile; it makes me happy.

The song, "Fix You," begins, and I cheer and shout, excited to hear one of my favorites. I reach up, wanting to tell him thank you, but he turns around and kisses me, sitting down to place me on his lap. He doesn't let our lips disconnect in the process. I'm a little surprised. Our last conversation left me confused about our whole relationship. It's the first time he's kissed me since the incident on his bedroom floor.

"How can a person be this beautiful inside and out?" he murmurs. His hand is in my hair, and he's gently stroking my cheek with his thumb. It's apparent he likes to hold my face. When he lifts his lashes, he pierces me with those beautiful eyes of his. There's a tenderness about him that has me so entranced, I almost forget where I am.

Feeling the butterflies flutter wildly in my belly, I blush then turn away, finding a group of women staring at us. This public display of affection is new to me. I'm not sure if I like the daggers directed my way. I Flick my gaze back to Luke. "We have an audience."

His fingers graze my shoulder, down my arm, to the palm of my hand then slowly back up. He doesn't even bother to spare them a glance. "Ignore them."

Ignore them. I wish it were that simple, but I'm not used to attracting attention, and I'm pretty sure one of them just flipped me off. It's hard to ignore, but I give a shy smile before the crowd gets loud and "Speed of Sound," begins to play. Leaning over, I press my mouth to his ear and say, "Thank you for bringing me. You have no idea how much this means." I grab his hand to pull him up then sway to the beat of the music, while he stands behind me. Everything sounds so much better live, and I love that we're here.

"Excuse me," a high pitch voice shouts from somewhere behind me, then I'm shoved a few feet forward. I'm not sure if it is on purpose. I turn to find a woman in a tight black mini dress, with hair that reminds me of Barbie. Her heels have got to be six inches in height. She's tall, really tall ... and her legs could go on for miles.

I suddenly feel underdressed and maybe a little bit envious. Sure, I've seen beautiful women before, but this one is having a conversation with the man I was just kissing, and from the looks of it, she's on a mission.

I watch her seductively place a hand on his chest, then rise on her tiptoes as she speaks into his ear. He frowns, but she doesn't back off in the least. If anything, she gets closer. I can't hear what she's saying, but I can guess it's something inappropriate, especially since he came with a date. It hits me that I was shoved on purpose. The way she's hanging on him is a little surprising; she doesn't seem to mind that he's fighting her off, even though he's trying to be a gentleman about it.

I envision myself swinging her by her hair, playing it off like a crowd surfing incident gone wrong. She steps away; batting her lashes, she runs her pretty little manicured nail down his chest. *Oh. Hell. No.* I take a step toward her and poke my finger into her back. I do it hard for extra effect. It's not that I plan on fighting her. I'm just not going to stand here and take her crap any longer.

She spins around and slowly gives me a once over then flips her hair. Her aqua-colored eyes turn cold, with obvious disapproval. "Is there a problem?" she shouts.

I lean back and glare. "Yes, actually, there is a problem."

"Well, you can have him in a minute, sweetie. I'm not finished with him yet." She flashes a quick smile, and disregards me like I'm trash, turning back to rub her big fake tits against him. I'm shocked by her persistence.

"Can you not see that I'm with someone," he growls. "Leave us alone."

She turns around and stares at me. "You're really here with her? Meaning you drove with her," she yells.

"Yes. He actually drove with me," I say back. Seriously, who this chick? Some kind of obsessed stalker? No means no, regardless if you're a guy or a girl … right? She places her legs so that she's straddling one of his thighs and starts moving her hips, sort of like she's dry humping him.

"Get off me!" Luke flinches. It's obvious she's pushing his buttons. He's usually pretty calm and collected. Right now, though, there's no hiding that he's pissed, but his anger doesn't seem to have an effect on the woman's choices. She makes a pouty face, but barely backs away. Now I know Luke's not the type of guy who would ever hit a girl, so I decide to take matters into my own hands.

I finally intervene. Reaching out to tug on her long beautiful hair, I get her attention. I don't really know what I'm thinking. All I know is that I've had enough. "Did you hear what the man said?" My voice comes out as a growl, and I clench my teeth. "Please keep your hands, and your girl parts, off my date." I'm not even sure if you would call it that, but since we were making out five minutes ago, I'm confident enough to say it is. In all my life, I've never been in a girl fight, but I'm pretty sure something's about to go down with Little Miss Crazytown.

"You think you're special?" she replies in a hiss. "That you're the only one he wants?"

"Shut up, Vanessa! Don't you fucking talk to her like that!"

She gives a sarcastic chuckle, as she gets in my face. "What are you going to do? Hurt me?" She's looking right at me, but the question is for Luke.

"No. I'm not going to hurt you." Luke watches me. "But Reese over here will kick your ass."

"I'd like to see her try," she says, bringing her face even closer. "You're a homely little thing. Aren't you?"

Luke places his hands on my shoulders. "Don't listen to her. She's being a bitch." Glancing at Vanessa, he says, "Do me a favor and keep your bullshit to yourself."

She looks back and forth between us. "Do you always do her dirty work for her?"

"Reese can handle her own business."

She arches a brow. "Oh, I'm sure."

"Hi Luke." Another scantily dressed woman walks over. Judging by the look in her eyes, she knows him. *Perfect! They all know each other. How fun … probably had a big orgy.* Loosening up his hold on me, he nods his head. *Yep … definitely know each other.*

I move my eyes to the crazy chick's face, and she grins. "See?" Quickly flicking her gaze to her friend then back to me, she says, "He'll be done with you by morning." Then, she spits on me— literally *spits* on me.

I snap and launch at her, slipping out of Luke's hands onto the filthy floor of the arena. He's yelling my name, but I don't care. When he tries to pull me off her, I give him a warning, "I swear, you better let me take care of this!" Then I swing at her cheek as she raises an arm to block me, but it doesn't work. I get a good punch in, and she moves to a perfect position for me to break her arm, but I want to drag this out a little. The crowd parts around us as we yank, scratch, punch, and roll. My body explodes with adrenaline when she slaps at my face, and I pin her down, sitting on top of her.

"Girl fight! Girl fight! Girl Fight!" People are chanting. It only seems to encourage us more. Digging her fingernails deep into my breast, she squeezes the skin at my nipple. I stifle a cry. It stings like hell, but if she wants to fight like a girl, then I'll fight like one with her. I reach down and give her a dose of the pain I felt a second ago.

"You bitch!" she hisses, reaching for me. I dodge her fingers at the same time my shirt rips in her other hand. I feel several hard blows against my back, and spot a shoe aiming straight for my head. Instinctively I grab it, causing the owner to fall flat on her face when I twist it backward. I recognize her as another friend from her group when she sits up, and a small stream of blood trickles down her nostril. I think she's had enough, but she flies on top of me and starts swinging wildly.

I hook my legs around her back and give her a sweep, quickly flipping her on her back, holding her down with my knee. "Have you had enough?" I yell. "This is between me and psycho Barbie over there. No one else." She nods her head, and I get off her, watching her crawl away. I bring my attention back on the person I have the problem with who's currently trying to choke me. I can't believe this is actually happening.

I spin around and easily wrestle her to the ground, sitting on her torso. "Why'd you have to go and ruin a perfectly good night?"

There's commotion in the crowd as the song, "Yellow," plays in the background. "I mean … I love Coldplay!" I shout. "And you spit on me! What the hell!"

She flashes a grin, looking pretty banged up in the process. "When he's with you tonight …" Her eyes move to my left. When mine follow, I find Luke restraining her friends, who look like they're ready to jump me. "It'll be my face he sees."

"Out of the way. Security." *No way is she getting the last word.* Not only is this my very first girl fight, it's the first time I've ever been spit on, and let me say, it's disgusting.

I turn and face her. "I'm afraid you're mistaken." I grin. "You see, you're not really his type."

She arches a brow. "You mean the *'every man's fantasy'* type?"

Giving her a right hook to the chin, I knock her out cold and lean down so I'm inches from her face. "No," I pause, catching my breath. "I mean the unconscious type."

Chapter Twenty-Five

Reese

"I can't believe you got us thrown out of a Coldplay concert." After inspecting my body from head to toe, Luke hasn't shut up about the fight. It's like I'm trapped inside a car with a ten-year-old boy, and the twinkle in his eye is starting to bug me.

"Hardy har har! Real funny," I say, glancing at his shirtless body. "Again, thank you for the shirt, and thank you for letting me fight my own battle."

"After that death glare you gave me? I didn't have a choice." He laughs softly. "Plus, someone had to hold back the other girls." Gripping the steering wheel with one hand, he reaches over and pats me on the thigh. "You were like a little ninja out there." He flashes his dimples. "That was pretty badass, what you did."

"You think?" I crinkle my nose, watching him suspiciously. He knows the questions are coming. Even his chipper mood isn't enough to distract me.

"You took two of them down," he says enthusiastically. "Of course, I don't know why I'm surprised. You learned from the best." The corner of his mouth tips.

"Conceited much?" I'm ready to discuss how he knows the girls from the concert. I assume it's a topic he'd rather avoid. But I don't want to avoid it. I'm feeling a little confrontational. The five-minute squabble wasn't enough. The thought of Luke putting his hands all over either of them fills my body with jealousy and rage. What is it that they have that I don't? I mean, so what if I don't look like Malibu Barbie. At least I have a brain. I watch him pick up his phone, punch in a couple numbers then place it to his ear.

"Malibu Barbie?" he asks, glancing out of the corner of his eye.

Did I say that out loud? I don't care. I'm pissed and my boob hurts! So I ignore him.

He sets his phone down as we pull into the garage. "Logan wants to hang out." Turning off the ignition, he asks, "Have you met ..." he pauses, "... never mind."

I stare out the passenger side window before opening the car door. "No. I haven't met any of your friends—aside from the classy group I met tonight, and they jumped me." There's a heavy bag hanging in the right side of the garage. I walk over and punch it. When it swings back I hit it again, but my hand bends unnaturally. I grab my wrist and squeeze, clenching my jaw to hide the pain.

"Reese." He sighs. "What are you doing?"

I'm throwing a jealous tantrum. What does it look like I'm doing? Turning my back to him, I walk through the door, but he's right on my heels.

"Are you hurt?"

Are you kidding me? "Am I hurt?" My head snaps back, and I'm seething. "Don't act like you don't know why I'm upset!"

He closes his eyes.

"It's obvious you all knew each other. You knew each other pretty damn well!"

"Yeah, so what?"

"So what? Are you serious?" I glare.

"Go ahead. Ask me." His eyes burn into mine. "What do you want to know?" He follows me to the point that I'm pressed against the bathroom door. "That I'm a male whore?" he says a little louder. "I'm sorry if that surprises you. Maybe I wanted to keep my sex life to myself. Is that wrong?"

Oh, now he's just being an ass. I grab the handle and back into the bathroom. "You're right. Your sex life isn't any of my business, but feel free to ask me about mine. Then again, I've already told you everything." I slam the door ready to cry, but gasp when I see my reflection.

I look pathetic. My hair is all over the place. It's as if a bird flew in and made itself a nest and had a little party. There are streaks of mascara underneath my eyes and smeared across one of my cheeks. I count four blazing scratches starting at the top of my jawline and ending at the nape of my neck. I step closer to the glass then take off Luke's shirt, finding a patch of dry blood above my nipple. *Gross.* When Luke said *badass,* this was not what I was expecting. I kind of hoped I walked away unscathed. "Some badass," I murmur.

A light knock sounds at the door before Luke's velvety voice breaks through. "C'mon Reese. I'm sorry. Don't hide in the bathroom all night."

Please ... I'm not afraid to face him. I just don't want him to see me crying over him. Relieved when I spot the charcoal towel hanging on the rack, I scurry over and turn on the water. "I'm not hiding, Luke. It's called a shower."

"I put a clean towel in there," he says a little louder.

"I see it. Thank you." I stand at the door and wait for him to leave, knowing he's still on the other side.

"Do you hate me?" he asks, and I pause, debating on whether to answer. He's really good at getting what he wants so I try to make him suffer. "I know you're there," he says, sounding like a sad little boy.

I cave and open the door a fraction of an inch. "Can I help you? I'm trying to take a shower."

He leans against the wall, furrowing his brows. "Tell me if I'm wrong." He tilts his head to the side. "Am I being punished for my past?" So he did sleep with her ... or them. My stomach flips. I don't know how to reply to that, so I give him the only response I can think of. "What ever do you mean?" Okay, maybe I'm being a smartass, but I can't help it.

"Don't get cute. You know what I mean." He steps closer, looking directly into my eyes, as I fake disinterest. "You want to know the truth?" Without giving me any time to answer he says, "I slept with them. As a matter of fact, I slept with all of them."

I flinch, sucking in a breath. *All of them? How many were there? Five or six?* I can't look at him. So I shut the door in his face. Even though I already expected he'd been with at least one of them, it hurts to hear the words leave his mouth. "Thank you for sharing that wonderful piece of information with me, Luke," I tell him through the door. "If you're trying to hurt me, I assure you, you've succeeded."

"That's what I mean, Reese. It's my past, and you're judging me for it. It's not something I'm proud of, but I can't undo it." He pauses then says, "What's done is done. Shit! I'm not trying to hurt you. Do you really think that low of me? That I would be that selfish?"

I get what he's saying, and I shouldn't be so hard on him for his past. But I'm jealous, hurt, and confused, and I don't know how to put my feelings into words. Opening the door a second time, I leave just a sliver of a space where he can see me.

He's sitting on the floor with his legs sprawled out, his bare back against the wall, and his hair in a disheveled mess. He still manages to look beautiful. "That's not why I'm hurt, Luke." The steam filling the bathroom brings beads of sweat to my neck.

He lifts his lashes searching my face.

"I'm hurt because you gave them something that you'll never give to me. I'm hurt because those women have all seen a part of you that I won't get to see." I shrug. "I'm jealous."

His cheeks flush, and his brows rise to his hairline.

"I'm not talking about your penis, Luke! It's a whole lot more than that!"

He clears his throat, "I didn't say you were." Pursing his lips, he quickly looks away. *He totally thought I was.*

"I'm talking about your vulnerable side. The side you won't share with me. You won't talk about your past or your family, and when it comes to you and me," I stop. "What are we Luke? What's happening between us?" I point a finger. "Don't answer. Hold that thought." I quickly grab the towel and wrap it around my torso then open the door.

When he sees me, he sighs. "First of all, those girls know nothing about my family or my past."

I interrupt, "You slept with them ... every single one of them, yet you won't even touch me."

"God Reese, how many times do I have to explain it to you?" he groans, scrubbing his face with his hands.

"A girl can only be rejected so many times, before it starts to wear her down. Really Luke, I get it. It just hurts."

His eyes flare. "No you don't get it! You don't understand how wrong you are." He stands up, and I get behind the door, preparing to shut it.

"Look, I'm done talking. The water is still running, and I need to get in." I close it softly then step into the shower and cry as quietly as I can. It's moments like these when I really miss my mom.

I've been tossing and turning for nearly an hour now, ignoring my thirst for water. After twenty minutes in the shower, my tearful breakdown was apparent on my face, so I walked straight into Luke's room and haven't seen him since. I glance in the mirror, hoping the puffiness has faded. It's humiliating enough that I poured out my soul. If I have any ounce of dignity left, I'd like to hang on to it.

I make my way over to the kitchen using my best attempt to avoid Luke's gaze. The heat of his body sends prickles down my spine when I realize he's standing close behind me. Two strong hands grip my shoulders then turn me so I face him.

"Will you stop being dramatic and give me a chance to talk?" His voice is soft, but his words manage to piss me off.

My eyes lift to his. "I. Am. Not. Being. Dramatic!" Okay, maybe I am, but so what? I try to walk away, but his firm grip holds me in place. "Let go of me," I hiss.

The shift in his gaze says he knows I've been crying. He clenches his jaw then slowly breathes through his nose before he says, "I don't know how to do this." Letting go of one of my shoulders, he points between him and me. "These feelings between us. The feelings I have for you, I don't know what to do with them."

I arch a brow. "What does that even mean?"

"God, Reese, I don't know!" he yells. "Can't you see this is hard for me?" He places his hands on his hips. "I'm trying to protect you. It's just … it's complicated."

I throw my arms up. "Oh, it's complicated all right! With you, it's always complicated." I get in his face. "Do me a favor, let me know when you've got it all figured out. But I promise you, I may not be around when you do." I turn around and storm down the hall toward the bedroom.

Right before I get to the door he says, "I don't want to hurt you."

"Too late," I yell back. I slam the door shut and hop into bed.

Chapter Twenty-Six

Reese

If this isn't a dream, then I'm waking to the most beautiful creature I've ever seen. He's sitting on the edge of the bed watching me with so much intensity. I swear I could get drunk off of the cognac that are his eyes. When my pulse begins to race, I can't keep the smile from stretching across my face. I'm done fighting. I want to lay here and take all of him in.

"I want to show you something," he says, his voice sounding a little shaky. I nod my head as his hand reaches for mine.

"Feel." He brings my fingers to a circular scar I didn't notice before. It's on the lower part of his side, directly across from his belly.

"I walked in on my father smacking my mom around." Glancing over his shoulder he says, "She was small like you, you know, petite." His eyes flick to the floor. "I jumped on his back, thinking I could stop him, but he was stronger and launched me off. I was nine," he gives a short laugh. "It was the first time I had the balls to stand up to him." He brings his gaze back to the scar. "I thought he was going to kill me, but he had other plans."

I cringe, thinking the plans involve torturing his son then squeeze his hand so he'll continue. It's hard to hear what he went through, but the fact that he's telling me is progress.

"I tried to get to my mom, but he grabbed me and held me still. I'll never forget the sound. My skin was sizzling." he chokes out.

"God Luke, that's awful …"

"You're telling me," he replies as he nudges me. "Sure you want the rest?"

"I'm sure." I give a half grin when he lifts his brows in question. "I'm serious. I want to know."

He watches me carefully, but finally continues. "So he lit another one and put it out right here," he says, tapping his thigh— an area that's always covered when I'm around him.

"Can I see?" I ask, no longer holding the tears at bay. I can't help it. He's finally opening up. The combination of his vulnerability and his story makes me cry.

He stands and pulls down his pants, revealing the black boxer briefs underneath them. I run my hand over the scar. It's nearly identical to the one on his side. "There's another one I want you to feel." He pulls up his jeans then grabs my fingers. "Do you feel that?" he asks, pressing them against his scalp.

There's a dip right in the center. "I feel it."

"I was fourteen. My father had my mom in a chokehold. He put her head through a wall before I could stop him. After I got a few punches in, he threw me through the sliding glass door. I was bigger, but still no match for him. There was glass everywhere." He taps the spot of the old injury.

"I'm so sorry," I say, feeling a tear slide down my cheek.

His face falls. "This is why I don't like to tell you these sort of things. See? I already got you crying again," he says softly, eyes blazing into mine.

I shake my head back and forth. "I just don't understand. How can anyone be so cruel?"

"You don't know my father." He shrugs. "Anyway, it's more common than you think. There isn't a way to understand it."

"Is that why you were put into foster care?" Maybe I've overstepped my boundaries, but I'm dying to know.

"One of the reasons," he pauses, "My father was in and out of prison. But nothing would ever stick. My sister and I'd go back and forth, getting placed in different homes." He sighs. "Jim and Pam were the last. We just bonded differently I guess. There was something distinctive about them." He shrugs. "That's around the time I saw you."

"I didn't know," I murmur.

"You met my buddy, Logan, that night at the club. Remember? Or were you too hammered by that point?"

I remember, but barely. "Yeah." I roll my eyes. "I remember."

He lifts his brows. "Despite what happened, Logan's pretty legit. He's a good guy, just needs a little help in the lady department." The corner of his mouth curves.

You should talk, I want to say, but instead I keep my mouth shut.

"When my sister and I were first released into the system, it was Logan's family that took us in. Both of us," he adds. "Then his father passed away unexpectedly, and things went to shit from there, especially for Lauren."

I tilt my head, confused. "Where was your mother during all of this? Was she involved?" If she were anything like my mom, I wouldn't put it past her.

"They'd usually book her on child endangerment charges and declare her an unfit parent." He glances at me. "They didn't like that she was protecting him. Regardless of her reasoning."

This whole conversation makes me uneasy, so I nervously chew on my nails. "Why'd she do it?"

He leans forward. "She was scared." Resting his elbows on his knees, he continues, "She was scared for all of us."

"Scared of what?"

"My father and what he was involved with."

"I don't understand. Couldn't you have gone to the police?"

"The police?" he snorts. "The police were part of it. We didn't know who we could trust."

I gasp. "But you said they didn't like her protecting him. Why wouldn't they like it, if they were involved?"

"Not all were involved, but there were several. Money can make people do things, especially when they're dealing with the cartel," he adds, shrugging. "When your life, or your family's life, gets threatened …"

"Wait. Wait. Wait. The cartel?" I ask, narrowing my eyes. "As in the Mexican Drug Cartel?"

"As in the Mexican Drug Cartel," he confirms, just when I thought it couldn't get any worse.

I suck in a breath. "Was my father involved?" *Please God don't tell me he was.* "I mean … do you know?"

He leans over and tucks my hair behind my ear. "He wasn't involved, Reese."

I sigh in relief. "Thank God. I don't think I could handle it if you told me he was."

He lifts my chin. "He doesn't seem so bad after hearing my story. Does he?" His voice is soft. He's right, but who would, after hearing what Luke just told me?

"No. I guess he doesn't. That's not saying much, though." I rub my fingers over the scar on his side. "I don't like that he hurt you."

He watches me carefully then stops my hand with his own. "I don't like that *I hurt you*," he says softly. The look in his eyes renders me speechless. "I heard you last night. I hate that I make you cry." He lifts his lashes. "I can't fight it anymore."

The desperation in his words makes me feel tingly inside. "Fight what?" I ask quietly.

"What I feel for you." He leans in and gives me a gentle kiss. "What I've felt since the first day I saw you again." He grips my hair and scoots me back on the bed, placing himself on top of me.

His words confuse me, but my heart seems to understand. "The first day you saw me again? But, you said you thought I was a kid!" I barely squeak out. I try to look at him, but his face is nestled deep in my neck.

He chuckles. "I told you. I was fighting it."

"And you're not fighting it anymore?"

He lifts his face to look into my eyes. "Nope," he replies adorably.

My eyes fall on his dimples. "Well, what about my feelings?" I arch a brow, watching his grin fade.

"Feel what you want," he growls. "I'm not going anywhere. You're stuck with me."

"I am? I mean … you're not?"

"I'm not." he kisses me again.

"What if I have another date? Are you going to come along with us?"

There's a shift in his gaze when he answers. "Whatever it takes to convince you that you're mine, I'll do it." His eyes pierce into mine. "I'm all in. And I don't share."

I'm surprised by his seriousness. "There's no need for convincing." I say softly. "I know who I want." I smile, and he slowly grins back.

Chapter Twenty-Seven

Reese

"There's a man standing at Luke's front door," Gia shouts from somewhere in our newly shared condo. We've been rooming together for close to a month now. Tonight we plan on celebrating with a barbeque and a couple of handsome men.

"It's not the hot new neighbor, is it? Luke likes to be discreet. That's what the property management company is for." He rented out one of his condos to a man who Gia thinks looks identical to David Beckham. She's been dying to see if I agree, but I haven't had the chance to see him—not that it really matters. I always seem to be working when he makes an appearance.

"Nope, someone else. He was peeking through the windows just a second ago."

"Our windows?" *Huh, that's weird.* After adding one last coat of mascara, I step back and stare at my reflection in the mirror.

"No, his." She pops her head in the bathroom. "Maybe you should see what he wants. But first, look at my dress. Do you like it?" We introduced Gia and Logan the day after my mom left. It was also the first time I'd seen him since that night at the club. Aside from giving Luke a hard time about being whipped, he was a pretty good sport, and managed to leave me alone. His main focus was on Gia. They hit it off immediately.

I close the tube and put it away, then eye her sparkly, one-shoulder dress, dropping my gaze to her matching pumps. She looks amazing. "A little overdressed for a barbeque, don't you think?" I grab a Q-tip to wipe the black smudges off my eyelids. "Either way you look great."

"There's no such thing as overdressed. Besides, I'm curious to see Logan's reaction."

I pull away from the mirror and look at her again. "He'll be panting when he sees you. He's bad enough as it is."

"You think?"

"Oh, come on. You could have your head in a towel and a green mask on your face, and he would still think you look hot."

She gasps. "I'd never allow him to see me like that."

I look down at my casual attire: my favorite pair of jeans and oversized red sweatshirt. The weather's finally cooler, and I usually choose comfort over sexy. "Can you see if that man's still there?"

She prances toward the window and sneaks a peek through the blinds. "Yep," she says over her shoulder.

"I guess I'll go see what he wants." I make my way to the door, instantly having his attention when I open it. "Hi." I smile, making my best attempt at being polite. Right away I notice there's something *off* about him. "Luke ran up to the store. Is there anything I can help you with?" As he takes several steps in my direction, I notice he's handsome and older.

"Who are you?" His voice is familiar. He's at least six feet tall with salt and pepper hair and a medium build. The way his eyes travel my body is a little unnerving.

"I'm sorry," I say, reaching out my hand once he's close enough. "I'm Reese, Luke's girlfriend." I'd be lying if I said I didn't feel all warm inside when those words left my mouth. I'm having a hard time getting used to it.

His eyes light up, and it takes a minute before he shakes it, although it takes even longer for him to let go. "I'm Glenn." His thumb runs across the back of my hand giving me chills ... and not the good kind. "Luke's father."

My breath catches, and my entire body freezes. The sparkle in his eyes says he knows I'm already aware of him. "Hello," is all I manage to reply. I don't want to be afraid of this man, but I am. There's some sort of hold he has on Luke, and it's obvious he's scared of him, too, which says a lot.

"Girlfriend, you say?" He cocks a brow. Oh God, I hate to admit it, but with that expression, he looks just like his son.

I want to tell him he's a monster—remind him of the pain he put his children through, but I can't get out the words. I can't manage to say anything. So instead, I nod in a confused daze.

"Is that a yes?"

"Uh yeah, it's a yes," I reply, pulling myself together. "It's just that, you and Luke look so much alike. It's a surprise to me, that's all."

"You think so?" He steps a little closer, and the smile that spreads on his face is pure evil.

I should have pressed Luke harder for information about this man. We've been so consumed with Gia's and my moving, that we never further discussed the subject. I may just have to kick his father's ass if he gets any closer. I tuck my hair behind my ear. "Most definitely."

"Well, I guess I should take that as a compliment. Does he share, or does he keep you all to himself?"

My cheeks flush. "Excuse me?" I can't believe he actually just said that. I clear my throat because it's now gone dry. "That's an inappropriate thing for you to say, and it's really none of your business."

"Well, look at that. You're red as a tomato." He ignores me.

"Just talked to Logan. The boys are on their way," Gia calls. When I turn around, she's already gone, leaving the door wide open.

I clench my fists, wanting to strangle her for shouting that information, then turn back to face Glenn. "I better get going. I'll tell Luke you came by," I say, pointing behind me. "Looks like dinner's almost ready." Okay, so dinner isn't anywhere close to ready. The boys are coming back with the hamburger meat, and they still have to grill, but I want this man out of here and far away from Luke.

"Are you nervous?" He arches a thick brow, and I cover my reddened cheeks.

"What … this? Probably just too much sun." I wave it off, not wanting to give him the satisfaction.

"No, I don't think that's what it is. You're shy. I know a shy woman when I see one." He looks over my shoulder. "Is this your place?"

I follow his gaze and sigh, wishing he would leave, then get a direct view of Gia, placing white flowers on the table.

Without invitation, he walks around me, straight into our condo. My mouth drops, and I follow behind. Normally, in a situation like this, I'd break his nose, or knee him in the balls, but this is Luke's father. I really don't know what to do. Even though I don't like him, I can't bring myself to hurt him. As unsettling as this man is, part of me wonders if he's here to apologize. I mean, my father seems remorseful for his actions, so maybe, just maybe, Glenn does, too. But maybe it's wishful thinking on my part. I watch him walk right up behind Gia, and she turns around, giving him her signature smile.

"Hello. You must be …"

"Gia." Her eyes flick to me then back to him. "Her roommate and best friend, but not in that order."

I silently try to communicate with her, but she furrows her brows, looking at me as though I'm a puzzle she can't figure out. She doesn't know a thing about Luke's father. I didn't feel it was my place to tell her.

"Glenn Ryann. Lovely to meet you, Gia," his all too familiar voice replies.

Her smile grows and her eyes widen. "You're Luke's father?"

"The one and only."

She giggles. "Of course! I can totally see the resemblance. Are you going to stay?"

Before she can finish, I interrupt her, "It's getting late. I'll let him know you came by. Is there a message you'd like me to pass along?" He tilts his head, cleverly smirking at me. He has me figured out. It's become obvious he's not here to apologize. The more I watch him, the more ready I am to call my father, and tell him I'll give him another chance. I'm beginning to understand what Luke was talking about.

Gia scolds me with her eyes. "I'm sure the boys bought enough meat to share. They'll be here any minute." She turns back to Glenn. "Why don't you stay for hamburgers?"

There are times when a friend can tell what the other is thinking, just from a simple look. Unfortunately, this is *not* one of those times.

Glenn's gaze falls on me when he responds, "I'd love to stay."

"Wonderful," Gia responds. "Can I get you something to drink? A beer? Water? Some iced tea?" Her eyes flick to mine, and she frowns. She'll find out soon enough that she's the one that should be getting frowned at.

"A beer sounds nice."

Gia nods. "Go ahead and make yourself at home." She gestures toward our sitting room. "I'll be right back with your beer." She turns around and strides into the kitchen. I want to follow, but there's no way I'll leave him unattended.

Snapping me out of my thoughts, Glenn says, "I have to admit, they keep getting prettier." When I glance at him he adds, "It's about time my son went for a curvy brunette." I try to block out his words, but my curiosity gets the best of me. "Tall, blonde, and very thin," he grimaces. "That was his usual flavor." Resting his chin in his hands, he says, "But me, I prefer them more like you ... curvy."

"I don't care," I snap, even though I do. It hurts to hear I'm the exact opposite of Luke's usual preference.

"I love brunettes," he murmurs.

"Gee, I'm flattered."

"You have a mouth on you, too. You'll need to be trained."

I arch a brow. "I'll need to be what?"

"You're different than the others." He lightly taps his finger against his lips. "Maybe he's more like his father than I realized."

"Well, I can definitely see a strong resemblance," Gia murmurs, cheerfully walking into the room, handing Glenn his beer. "And your son is crazy about this girl over here," she adds, flashing her sparkling smile.

God Gia, would you just shut up? I roll my eyes, wanting her to quit while she's ahead, but she won't even glance my way. She's completely oblivious to the damage she's causing.

"I don't doubt that he is," he replies, but he looks right at me as he says it. "I assume you haven't been intimate with each other yet?" He puts an emphasis on the word *intimate*, and I glare.

"You're sick! That's none of your business."

He presses his beer to his lips. "That's where you're wrong." Taking a swig, he swallows then replies, "My son. My business."

"Okay, this is awkward," Gia says loud enough for both of us to hear.

I walk over to the door and open it. "You need to leave."

This time, Gia doesn't argue; instead she stands right beside me, still as a statue, as we watch Glenn take another sip. "I don't know what's going on, Mr. Ryann." One of her hands takes mine. "But you should probably go." I give it a squeeze, relieved we're finally on the same page here.

"Why don't we wait and let my son decide?" he replies, resting an arm over the back of the couch. That's when two familiar voices, and the sound of footsteps echo not far from the entryway.

Chapter Twenty-Eight

Reese

Luke walks in with his hands full of groceries. Logan follows a few steps behind. They chat away, placing their bags on top of the counter. Gia and I stand quiet, both of us afraid of what's to come.

"You girls smell good, or at least one of you does," Logan says, grinning. "You two hungry? I'm fucking starving."

"Use your manners, man. Not around the women," Luke tells him, swatting the back of his head.

Logan opens a bag of chips then shoves a handful into his mouth. "Sorry bro, I forgot."

"Reese always smells good," Luke replies lazily. "Good enough to eat." He brings his eyes to mine then his expression quickly changes. "What's wrong?" He makes his way over and carefully lifts my chin. His eyes are full of concern. "Are you okay?"

"Behind you," Gia answers, after a quick clearing of her throat. Something flashes in his features, then he narrows his gaze, slowly turning to face his father.

"What the fuck are you doing here?" he roars grabbing him by the collar. *So much for not saying the 'F word' around the women.*

"Calm down, son," Glenn replies in a hushed, relaxed tone. It only seems to piss him off more.

"Don't call me that! Don't you call me your son!" His glare is lethal as he grips him tighter. "Did you touch her?" His eyes flick to my face. "Did he touch you?"

I hold my hands out to calm him, shaking my head *no*. "I'm okay, Luke. He didn't touch me. I promise." I've never seen him this upset. It hurts to see him like this.

He looks at Gia. "Is she telling the truth? Did he touch either of you?" The desperation in his face rips me apart.

"He didn't touch us. We're fine," Gia says. That's when I notice Logan standing in front of her protectively. I have no idea how long he's been standing here, but regardless, I'm thankful he is.

"You need any help buddy, or you got this?" Logan asks.

With Glenn still firmly in his grasp, Luke says, "The girls don't need to see this." He points toward me, his eyes never leaving his father. "Keep an eye on that one."

"Hey!" I frown, folding my arms.

"We're taking this outside." Luke tilts his head. "Do you understand?"

Logan smirks. "I believe I do, bro." The question wasn't aimed at him. I'm pretty sure it was meant for Luke's father.

Luke loosens his hold, and they step toward the door. "Just so we're clear ..." He gets in his father's face. "I'll kill you if you go anywhere near her again. Do you hear me?" His father doesn't answer as the door shuts behind them.

It's obvious Luke's the stronger of the two, but Glenn fights dirty. He doesn't play by the rules, and that's what scares me the most. I make my way to the window and try to hear what they're saying.

"Excuse me," Gia says. "Is anybody going to tell me what's going on?" Logan and I exchange a glance. "What?" she asks, looking back and forth between us.

"Have I mentioned how incredibly sexy you look?" Logan replies, walking toward her with outstretched arms.

She gives him an authentic smile then quickly embraces him in a hug. "Thank you, but don't change the subject. This isn't exactly how I expected to spend the evening. What's going on with Luke's father, and why is everyone being so rude to him?" Her eyes land on me. "I know he's a bit of a perv, but does he really deserve *this* kind of treatment?"

"It's more than that," Logan replies.

"Obviously. And I'm sure you have good reason. Does it have any thing to do with the whole foster care thing?" Her brow arches.

I open my mouth to answer, then our gazes shift to the door, when the voices outside grow louder. I take a peek through the blinds, listening as they argue.

"You women are nosey."

I look over my shoulder and shoot daggers at Logan. "Shh. Be quiet. I'm trying to hear what they're saying."

"She's right. Shut up, Logan."

His eyebrows pull together. "Did you just tell me to shut up?"

I stare at them pleadingly. "Will you two *please* do this somewhere else? Seriously, I can't hear a thing."

"Maybe it's none of your business," Logan snaps.

Gia gives him a glare. "Don't talk to her like that!"

"I'm just watching out for my bro."

"And I'm just watching out for my girl."

I spin around, throwing my up my arms. "Really?"

Gia takes a couple steps back, reaching for Logan's hand. "We need to talk." She gives me a wink before he's following her down the hall like a lost puppy. *Thank God.* I move closer to the spot where Luke and his father are standing and press my ear against the window so I can hear better.

"I wish I was there to save her," Glenn says. "What happened to your mother was tragic. She was a good woman." I take another look, noticing they're standing only about a foot apart. Luke looks extremely agitated.

"C'mon. Do you really think I believe that? That you have regrets? That you ever feel guilty? You can quit the horse shit," Luke spits. "Cuz there's no way in *hell* I'm buying it." I want to run outside and hold him—help him get through this—tell him that he's not alone.

"I never said I felt guilty."

Luke gives a sarcastic laugh. "Are you fucking kidding me? She's dead because of you!"

"Don't get yourself worked up, son. Your neighbors just might call the cops," Glenn chides devilishly. "We wouldn't want that now, would we?"

"You think I give a shit? I'm their landlord! Get out of here, and leave us alone! Or I'll call the cops!" The fact that he just screamed he's everybody's landlord shows just how pissed he is. He doesn't like people to know he's the owner. He doesn't want to be bothered with it. It's the reason he hired a property management company.

"What is that going to do for you, son? I'm a free man now. And you still have a debt to pay." He grins. "I'm afraid I can't leave you alone until you pay it."

A debt to pay?

"I don't owe you shit!" he hisses, jabbing his finger into his father's chest.

Glenn chuckles. "Now you're making up stories. Did you think I'd forget? After all those years rotting in that cell?"

I watch Luke close his eyes as he pinches the bridge of his nose. "Look. Lauren and I don't want you here." He audibly sighs. "It's better if you just walk away and pretend we never existed."

"Better for whom?" Glenn questions, but Luke doesn't give him a response. There's a gleam in his eye when he stands tall and straightens his collar, finally breaking the silence. "That desert princess of yours sure cares a lot about you," he says in a low hum. The words are meant as a threat.

Uh oh. I jump off the couch, bolting toward the door, knowing he pushed Luke over the edge. When I step outside, he's shoving

Glenn against the house hard. "You keep away from her," his voice is deadly. "Do you understand me? Don't you even look at her," he seethes.

Glenn laughs wickedly, purposely resting his eyes on me, letting them linger. I guess he has a death wish. "It would be a shame if anything happened to her. Like your mother, you never know when an accident may strike."

Shocked by what he just said, my breathing picks up, and my heart thumps rapidly inside my chest. *Was his mother's death not an accident? Did Glenn kill her? Was it arranged?* Luke's slamming Glenn's head against the stucco wall. Over and over again he's shouting, "I'll kill you! I swear to God I'll kill you!" He's completely lost it.

A flood of tears stream down my face. "Luke, stop!" I scream. He doesn't hear me. "Please, just stop! You're killing him!" Blood is flying everywhere. I'm terrified if someone doesn't intervene, Luke will do exactly what he promises. I run to the door and push it open. "Logan! Logan, help! Logan, get out here! Please! I need you!" I don't see him anywhere. He's probably still in Gia's room.

I race over and try to place my body between them, putting a hand on each of their chests, hoping to push them apart, but it barely does any good. The two men are so much stronger. My eyes flick to Glenn, and an evil grin spreads across his bloody face. I'm surprised that he's still conscious and still putting up a fight, especially since he's lost a lot of blood. Desperately trying to separate them, I try to wrap my arms around Luke's neck, and instead get a hard elbow right in the jaw. Everything happens so fast when the contact sends me flying.

As soon as I hit the ground, Luke hovers over in me a panic. "What happened?" I can't answer. I can't even move my jaw, but I'm thankful for the distraction. I lift my lashes to meet his concerned gaze. "Are you hurt?" He looks me over carefully. "Did I hurt you?" He was in such a trance that he didn't even know who hit me. If I told him it was his father, it would defeat the whole purpose.

"I'm okay, really. You didn't mean to," my words barely audible with my jaw already starting to swell.

"You should really be more careful, son," Glenn's voice says in the distance. "She could have been seriously injured."

"Shut up," Luke yells, not looking back. "Nobody asked you." Moving my eyes to Glenn's bloody features, I can see he's unrecognizable. It's obvious he needs a hospital, but he doesn't seem like the type. I look back to Luke as he lightly brushes his thumb over my jaw.

"I should be going," Glenn says. Luke and I ignore him. "I think I'll have to decline on the dinner invitation. Maybe another time," his voice is wistful. "I'll be in touch." I could feel his gaze on me, but wouldn't return it. I just wanted to focus on the man kneeling in front of me, his eyes now filled with pain.

Luke scoops me up in his arms and carries me inside. I feel like a baby as he walks me down the hall into my bedroom. "Luke, I'm fine. It really isn't that bad, and you're bleeding." I watch a stream of blood trickle down his temple. You can definitely tell he was in an altercation, but he didn't look nearly as bad as his father.

"Lie down. I'll be right back." He places me gently on the bed, searching my face.

I can feel my jaw throbbing. "Stop staring at me like that. It's not as bad as it looks. I swear." He makes a face like he doesn't believe me then strides down the hall. I hear banging on what I assume to be Gia's door.

"Everything taken care of?" I hear Logan ask—there's some kind of music playing in the background. A moment later I hear a loud pop and Gia screaming.

"What the hell was that for man?" Logan yells.

"I asked you to keep an eye on my girl! She's sitting in there with a swollen jaw! Now you have one to match!"

"Shit! Is she okay?"

"Wait. What?" Gia asks.

"Mmm," Luke growls back before Gia's storms into my room.

"What happened to you?" She places her hands on her hips, narrowing her eyes. "Did someone punch you?"

"I tried to break them apart," I say then wince because it hurts to talk. "I'll give you the details later." Luke walks in with an ice pack. The blood on his face has dried, and I notice it's all over his shirt—most of it probably his father's. "Luke, you're a mess. Let me clean you up. I'm fine ... really." I reach for the ice pack, but he jerks it away, clenching his jaw like he's irritated.

"Lay down. Your jaw looks worse," he quietly says, then tucks me into bed, before he lightly presses the ice pack against my face. He strokes my hair with his other hand, furrowing his brows.

I attempt to smooth out the worry lines using my thumb. "It's not your fault, Luke. I thought you were going to kill him. I was scared." I pause, trying not to flinch from the pain my talking is bringing. I don't want him to worry any more than he already is. "I purposely stepped between you two, trying to stop you from making a horrible mistake."

"Would it have been?" he asks, watching me. His face is serious. "A mistake?" He presses his lips into a tight line. The fact he's even asking this has me stunned silent. He looks down at his clothes and sighs. "I'm going to go clean up ... do some thinking. I'll be back." He leans over and kisses me on the forehead. "Is there anything I can get you before I go?"

"What do you need to think about?" I reach out and grab his hand, spotting the blood on his knuckles. "You're making this a bigger deal than it is. So what? I caught an elbow in the jaw. I'm used to this kind of stuff. Its pretty much part of my daily routine." I give a weak smile.

He eyes me for a minute, then says, "It's a lot bigger than you think, Reese." Then he lets go of my hand and walks away, leaving me with nothing to say in response.

"Rise and shine beautiful." I'm lying comfortably in my bed when Luke's velvety voice awakes me from my slumber. We're supposed to catch a movie this afternoon. From the sound of it, he's in a good mood, which makes me happy. He's been acting kind of funny the past few days. I'm pretty sure it's related to everything that happened with his father. His hair tickles my face as he presses his soft lips to the crook of my neck, slowly kissing every spot.

"Good morning to you," I murmur, doing my best to hold in my breath since I haven't brushed my teeth yet. He smiles against my skin, bringing his lips to my eyes, then my nose, and around the line of my jaw. "Ow. Be careful," I wince, instinctively blocking my face with both of my hands. It's still feels tender, even though it has had a few days to heal.

"Shit! Did I hurt you?" He jerks away in a panic.

I reach up and grab his arm, focusing on his painful expression—one he's been wearing for the past few days. I try to give him the best smile I can muster. "I'm okay. I sort of overreacted for a second. There are parts that are still a little sore, but it's really not that bad," I say, hoping to convince him.

When I stand, he places his hands on my hips and brings his forehead to mine, closing his eyes. "Sometimes I wonder if it would have been better for you if I never walked back into your life." He clenches his jaw.

My heart drops into my stomach, and I back away from his grasp. "Why would you say that?" I ask him.

He looks deep into my eyes, not giving me an answer. He just watches me with the same intense expression for what seems like minutes. It makes me nervous, but it also makes me want to kiss him senseless. "Do you ever wonder?"

"Never. Not once has it crossed my mind," I immediately reply. "Just stay right there," I point. "This conversation is far from over, but I need to brush my teeth." He presses his lips into a tight line then sits on the bed and waits for me. "You need to stop worrying. You're really starting to make me nervous."

"You make it sound so easy," he replies sarcastically. "I'm going to go shower. I'll leave the door unlocked. The movie starts in an hour."

Chapter Twenty-Nine

It's been ten days since we've seen Luke's father, and things are far from back to normal. Logan and I are on the couch, eating a bowl of popcorn, as we watch our favorite *Supernatural* episodes. In a few minutes, I'll be making a phone call that could possibly change my life. I haven't been able to stay still, and Logan keeps glancing at me out of the corner of his eye like I'm annoying him. Usually it's the other way around.

"Are you on something?" he asks.

"Leave her alone, man. She's nervous." I turn and find Luke standing in the doorway in all of his glory. It still baffles me that this man is mine. His shirt fits a little tighter than what he usually wears, and his jeans are hanging low, but not *too low*. It looks perfect actually. I want to run my hands over the contours of his chest then press my lips against his belly—something I haven't done yet, but have thought about many times. The corner of his mouth tips, as he stares at my face. I wonder if he knows what I'm thinking. Part of me doesn't care. He already has me blushing with his intense gaze. "I see you're both able to chew again."

I throw a handful of popcorn toward him, and he flinches. "Is everything okay? You looked pretty stressed when you were on the phone. Who was that?"

"No one important." His eyes flick to Logan then back to me—something he's been doing a lot lately. "You ready?"

The butterflies I felt earlier swirl around in my stomach. I take a deep breath. "I'm ready." I hop off the couch, and he leans down to give me a gentle kiss.

"It'll be fine. I promise." He kisses me again, this time as if it's the last, and when he pulls away, I'm breathless. "Happy twenty-first birthday," he says softly.

"Can you two do that somewhere else?" Logan asks, throwing another handful of popcorn. It hits us in the face, but we grin and kiss again because it's fun to piss him off. Then we make our way down the hall.

"Make sure you clean that popcorn up," I yell back.

"Yeah, yeah, I'll clean up your mess," he replies sarcastically.

I don't know why I'm so nervous. It's not like we haven't spoken since he left my mother and me … and I handled it pretty well the time we saw each other at the restaurant. If I'm being honest, my pride has a little to do with it. He sought me out last time. Now I'm the one holding the phone in one hand and my father's business card in another. "Where did you say you found this?" I ask. "I swear I threw it away." I run my finger over the black lettering displaying my father's name: Andrew Johnson.

"It was in the dryer. You probably washed it on accident," Luke replies, sitting next to me on my bed. "Quit fidgeting," he says, nudging me. "It'll be fine. Call him."

I bite my lip and press the talk button on the phone. "I don't know if I'm ready to do this." I swallow. "Maybe I need more time."

He reaches over and tucks my hair behind my ear. "Do you want me to dial for you?"

"No!" I jerk the phone away. "I'll do it." I suck in a breath then slowly let it out. "I don't need you doing my dirty work for me."

"Good girl," he replies, softly chuckling. "Do you want me to stay, or would you like me to leave you alone?" Although I'd love him to stay, it's probably best I do this alone.

"You can go."

He nods his head then leans in to give me a small peck. "Do you know how brave you are?" He brushes his thumb and finger along my jaw.

"I don't feel brave. Not right now," I murmur. "I feel like a scared little girl." I give a weak smile.

"You were brave then, too." He grins. "You've always been a fighter. It's one of the things I love about you." Did he mean that in a literal sense? The heat rises to my cheeks, and I know I'm visibly blushing, but his expression doesn't change. "You sure you want to do this alone?"

I gaze deep into his eyes. "I'm sure." After he walks away, I'm acutely aware that I'm on my own. So I stare at the numbers for what seems like forever, then finally give up and dial. When I get to the last number, it takes a couple beats for me to get my finger to press it, but I do. Then I clear my throat and nervously hold the phone to my ear.

A big part of me is hoping that he doesn't answer. The other part just wants to get this over with. His voice answers on the third ring, and I become frozen, unable to speak.

"This is Andrew," he says. I recognize the sound, but yet, it's different. "Hello."

My mouth drops then I stutter. "Hel … Hello … Dad?" I can't believe I just called him that. I mean he is my dad, but he hasn't been around for years. It's an awkward situation, and when he answers, he seems happy to hear my voice."

"Reese? Is that you? Are you okay?" From what I can tell, his concern is genuine. Without even a thought I try to ease his worry.

"I'm okay, Dad. Everything is fine," I pause, as he sighs in relief. "I just wanted to tell you that I've thought about it, and I'm willing to give you a chance." An unwanted tear rolls down my cheek. "Can we … can we take things slow?"

"So what made you decide to do it?" Gia asks me. I just got home from Luke's. He cooked my favorite meal, and bought me several little presents, including the bottle of wine that Gia and I are sharing. The two of us are lying on our patio, in our jammies, gazing up at the stars. The weather is perfect tonight—right around seventy degrees, with a slight breeze that tickles our skin.

"That night with Luke's father made me realize that there are some people in this world who make mistakes and truly regret them. Then there are others who are just plain evil." I turn my head to the side so that I'm facing her, and she does the same. "My father regrets what he did." I shrug. "About a week ago, I decided it was time to forgive him. Then I discussed it with Luke, and he encouraged me to give him a call, and the rest is history."

"Wow! I'm amazed to hear you say that." Her eyes widen. "Are you going to meet up with him?"

I purse my lips. "It's possible. We're going to start off taking things slow, but we did have a nice talk. He apologized for everything he put us through, and I apologized for the way I treated him at the restaurant."

"I'm shocked. Seriously, I'm shocked!" She smiles. "Reese, I'm so proud of you."

I roll my eyes embarrassed. "Whatever. It's not a big deal."

"Are you serious?" She sits up. "Do you realize how much you've changed this year? How much you've grown?"

I think about it, tilting my head. "Not really."

"Then let me tell you. One," she ticks off her fingers, "you stopped supporting your mom and let her take care of herself."

"That wasn't my choice, though," I argued.

"But you've finally learned that she doesn't need you helping her all the time. She isn't dependent on you anymore, and that's a good thing. She's okay." I sit up and take a sip of my wine when she adds, "Secondly, you're dating. I never thought I'd see the day when that would happen." She grins.

"Neither did I." I smile back, feeling my cheeks heat, when just the thought of the person I'm *dating* enters my mind. Then I'm reminded of his recent behavior and the letter I found at his condo.

"And third," she says, snapping me out of my thoughts. "You finally swallowed your pride and accepted a gift from someone who wanted to help you. A huge gift might I add. Like a house." She chuckles.

"Very true." I grin, shifting my gaze to the stars. "Gia."

"Yes."

"There's something I've been wanting to talk to you about. It has to do with Luke."

"Is he still being weird?" she mumbles.

I blow out a breath. "Yeah, but I think it's more than that."

"*Okay*. What is it?" She furrows her brows. "Did you finally have sex?"

"Ahem. No," I choke, when my wine goes down the wrong pipe. "Not even close. We're waiting."

She frowns. "Waiting for what?"

"I don't know. The right time I guess?" I shrug. "He says this way, it'll be a new experience for both of us—the waiting for him and the sex for me."

"Huh," she says, bobbing her head. "That's kind of cool. I bet it's going to be really hard for you, though." She giggles. "No pun intended." I spit out my wine and laugh with her until we both have tears coming out of our eyes.

When I'm able to catch my breath, I say, "Back to what I was saying."

"Oh yes," she replies. "Sorry for interrupting."

I circle the rim of my glass with my finger. "He's gotten worse. Something's really off." I meet her eyes. "Have you noticed anything different when he and Logan are together?"

"Like what?"

I search my brain for several examples. "Whispering between them, secretive phone calls, looks, random mood swings. Little things like that?"

She twirls a piece of her hair, thinking. "Actually, I do remember them speaking quietly a few times, sort of off by themselves. I never thought anything of it, until now that you said it." She narrows her eyes. "What's going on? Are you worried that they're gay or something?"

I shake my head. "No. That's not it *at all.*"

"*Okay,* then what?"

I lift my lashes. "Remember the other day, when Luke and I went to see that movie?"

She nods. "Yeah."

"I found a letter lying open on the counter. He was in the shower. I wasn't snooping or anything. I was getting a drink and just happened to glance that way. The words just sort of stood out to me, and I had to read the whole thing."

"What did it say?" She frowns.

"It was from his agent or manager. He was offering Luke a large amount of money to go to Brazil and fight. It seems like a pretty big deal. They train there, live there, fight there—and from what I read, a whole team of American fighters are going."

She tilts her head. "You're thinking that's why he hasn't been himself?"

I shrug. "That's what I'm wondering. The thing is, when he came out of his room, I was waiting for him on the couch. I got up to give him a hug, and the letter wasn't there anymore. It was just gone. Now, it's a few days later, and he still hasn't mentioned, it. I'm beginning to wonder if he's trying to hide it from me."

"What would be the purpose in that?"

"I don't know! But it's really stressing me out," I growl.

"Maybe his behavior has nothing to do with the letter. Maybe he just threw it away, and you're turning it into something it isn't. What if he doesn't want to go at all?" she replies.

"Then why has he been acting so weird?"

"Could be P.M.S. Guys get it, too, you know."

I roll my eyes. "Oh, I almost forgot. That same day, he said, *sometimes he wonders if I'd be better off if he never came back into my life.* Then he asked me, *if I felt the same way.* Do you think he'd tell me if he wanted to go?" I pause. "He wouldn't keep that from me? Would he? What if he regrets his decision to stop fighting, and thinks I'm holding him back?"

She grabs one of my hands. "I think you're being paranoid over nothing. Talk to him about it." She narrows her eyes. "Otherwise it's going to eat you up inside." She tops off her wine then pours the rest into mine, and I'm suddenly wishing we had another bottle.

Chapter Thirty

Ugh. I think I had way too much wine last night. I open an eye and groan, as the sun beams straight through the cracks of the blinds, making the throbbing in my head feel worse. There's pressure weighing on my body. I drop my gaze to the tan, muscular arm flung over my stomach. *Luke.*

"Morning," he grumbles into the pillow. "Does that mean I should leave?"

I shut my eyes and wince. "It's not you. My head is just ..." I pause. "When did you get here?" Last I remember, I was alone and never heard him come in.

"It was late. You were already passed out," his voice is rough with sleep. I love the way it sounds.

"You've been doing that a lot lately." I rub my temples. "Is everything okay?" Maybe he'll bring up the letter. Ever since the night with his father, he's been coming here to sleep, and sleeping in the same bed is against the rules. It just makes it harder to keep our hands off one another. But we've broken it several times. I think it's a stupid rule anyway. I'm not the one that made it up.

Instead of answering, he lays his head on my stomach, and I run my fingers through his disheveled hair. When my shirt rides up, his warm breath tickles my skin, and a rash of tiny bumps appear. I squirm when he lightly brushes his thumb across them, before he's peppering my belly with soft kisses. Soon, I'm a quivering mess. "I'm going to get you something for your head?" he whispers.

"You're a tease," I murmur, a little breathless. "And don't ignore my question."

He's watching me from under his lashes, and I notice the heat in his gaze. "I'll be back." He pushes up on his forearms then kisses my forehead and makes his way to the door. My eyes stay on him the whole time, before I get up to brush my teeth and take a swig of mouthwash. I climb back into my bed, hoping he finishes what he started, but I know it's wishful thinking.

Moments later, he's back with three ibuprofen and a tall glass of ice water. "Drink up. It'll help." My eyes drop to his taut abs, and he softly chuckles. I guess I'm not so good at being discreet.

"Thank you. And next time you don't have to be so bossy." The corner of his mouth tips in his signature grin. Then I do what he says, set down my glass, and ask, "Are you going to tell me what's bothering you?" I grab his hand and pull him down next to me. "Tell me what's going on?"

He runs a hand through his hair and opens his mouth like he's going to speak then decides against it. Finally, he says, "Lets just enjoy each other right now, okay?" He scoots me back on the bed and lies down on top of me, nuzzling his face in my neck. It's a movement that normally brings me comfort, but his words do the exact opposite, so I lay there chewing on my lip, wondering when my heart will start again. "Just relax," he says.

"How can I relax when you say something like that?" I ask softly. I want him to pull back and look me in the eyes, but he doesn't. Instead he squeezes me tighter, keeping his face right where it is. I begin to wonder if he's doing it on purpose. So he doesn't have to look at me. "Will you look at me, please?"

When he does, it only confirms my suspicions. The distance in his gaze has me biting back tears, out of fear. I'm scared of what's to come. This past week and half has made me an emotional wreck. I need to know the truth about the letter. This guessing game is getting us nowhere, and my patience is wearing thin. "There's something you're not telling me, isn't there—something you're afraid to tell me. I can see it in your eyes." He watches me carefully, without giving a response, then a moment later he slowly nods his head, gently brushing his thumb down my cheek. He looks sad. I cup his face in my hands. "Are you afraid you're going to hurt me?"

He switches to a sitting position, resting his elbows on his knees, and I sit up and watch him. "I was waiting for the right time." He turns to me. "But I guess there never really is a right time. And yes, I'm afraid of hurting you."

"Try me." I scoot over next to him then take his hand and squeeze it, deciding now would be a good time to go ahead and bring up the letter. "Does this have to do with the letter?"

He furrows his brows. "Letter?"

"The letter from your agent … about Brazil. I was getting a drink of water. It was just lying there—open—on the counter." I rub his arm. "Did you think I wouldn't support you if you wanted to go? Is that it?"

Something flashes in his features then quickly fades away, confusing me. "The letter." He nods. "I wasn't sure how you'd take it." He stares at the floor. "I know how you are about people leaving." Turning to face me, he says, "You don't take it so well. I was worried you'd be upset."

Narrowing my eyes, I reply, "I support you, Luke. If you want to fight, then go fight. I want you to be happy. I'd never try to hold you back from something you love." I shrug. "I mean, yeah, I'm going to miss you, but I can visit, and we can talk over the phone. We'll work it out."

He shakes his head and swallows. "It's not that easy. They don't allow visitors, and I don't know when I'll be able to call. My schedule's going to be crazy." His statement doesn't sit right. *Visitors aren't allowed?*

"*Okay*, well I guess we'll figure that part out." I frown. "Call them. Tell them you accept the offer."

"I already did," he replies, his eyes stare straight ahead.

"Oh." It's a little late to hide the expression of shock and disappointment on my face. I'm sad he didn't come to me first before making his decision, simply out of respect. "So when are you leaving?"

"Friday." His eyes move to mine, and he tucks a loose strand of hair behind my ear. I'm at a loss for words.

Friday? Friday is only two days away. WTF? Tears prick the back of my eyes. I had no idea he'd have to leave so soon. Has he considered my feelings about this whole situation at all? I honestly don't think he has … clearly. Oh God, I need to talk to Gia. What did he expect me to do—schedule my whole life around him? Because I should be considerate of his needs. But who cares about mine. Right?

"Reese," he says softly. "Tell me what you're thinking?"

I flick my gaze to his. "What am I thinking?" Here goes. "I'm thinking I'm a little hurt that you waited until now to tell me all of this. It's a pretty big deal, Luke. And the only reason you told me is because I brought it up. Did you even think to consider my feelings at all?"

His face goes pale. "Of course I thought about your feelings."

"I don't think you did. I gave myself too much credit. Here I am wondering if I'm holding you back. I wanted to tell you I support you. But the truth is, your decision had nothing to do with me. You had already made it, and I was left in the dark. You were leaving anyway."

He closes his eyes. "Come on, Reese. Don't do this. Not right now." He rubs the space between his brows.

I glare. "When would you like me to do it, Luke? Friday? It's only two days away. Two days! Were you even planning on telling me? Or were you just going to leave?"

He clenches his jaw. "Look, I understand why you're angry; you have every reason to be." His eyes are watery, and it's hard to even look in them. It plays with my mind.

"Well, I'm glad you understand." I lift my brows and cross my arms. "Because that would have *really* sucked if you didn't." He growls, gripping the back of his neck. "Have you been playing me for a fool this whole time?" I shake my head. "Don't answer that. I don't want to know." I bite back a sob, as the lump grows larger in my throat.

"Why would you say that?" He reaches out and wipes a tear from my cheek, pressing his lips into a tight line when I flinch at his touch. "You mean everything to me." He sounds so sincere, but I'm not buying it—not anymore—not after this.

"I hope you realize my anger has nothing to do with your decision. I planned to stand behind you. I wanted this for you, do you understand?" I point then wipe away a few more tears. They won't stop coming.

Placing his hands on my shoulders, he pleads, "I need you to listen to me. You've got it all wrong."

"Let me finish!" I yell. "It's your priorities, and where I come on that list. I can't believe I thought I might even be a factor in your decision. What did you think was going to happen? You'd leave, without warning, and I'd have nothing better to do than wait around for the infamous Luke Ryann?"

That pisses him off. "Just let me explain and stop coming to your own conclusions?" he fumes then paces back and forth, tugging on his hair. "You've got this all wrong."

I turn away because I can't look at him anymore. "I understand what you meant when you said it would have been better if you had never walked back into my life," I say quietly because I'm sobbing.

"You wouldn't have had to hurt me. Now it's too late. I know you care about me, Luke—just not in the same way."

"Fuck! Would you just listen for one second?" he yells, and I flinch.

"You should go," I reply with my back facing him. A second later, there's a loud noise and then the sound of a slamming door.

Yesterday morning was the last time I saw him. Aside from a few trips to the bathroom, I haven't been able to get out of bed. What's the point? Everything that surrounds me reminds me of him: my room, his lingering scent, this entire condo. *That he gave me for free.* "For free! Who does that?" I say out loud then throw another tissue toward the wastebasket and miss yet again.

"Knock, knock," Gia says, making her way into my room. She went to the store to grab another box of Kleenex. "You need this?"

"Come in." I give her a weak smile. "Thank you."

"Were you talking to yourself just before I walked in?"

"Yep," I reply with a sniffle.

She sits on my bed, and grabs a pillow, placing it in her lap. We're both quiet for a minute before she decides to break the silence. "He's in love with you. You know. Maybe you should give him a chance to explain himself. Logan says he's a mess."

"Screw Logan!" I growl. "And you're wrong. He's not in love with me. Not even close."

"Hey!" She frowns. "Logan's a good guy. He didn't do anything to you."

I roll my eyes. "The man drives me crazy, especially now that he's sticking up for my liar ex-boyfriend."

"So he's a little immature and has his friend's back." She giggles. "But he means well, and he's hot … sweet even. And Luke is not a liar. He's just good at … keeping secrets."

"If you say so."

"I do. You should at least hear him out."

I give a short, sarcastic laugh. "Now you're starting to sound like Luke. What is with you two?"

She shrugs her shoulders. "Maybe we see things a little differently than you do. I'm not saying that we're right and you're wrong. Oh! That reminds me," she snaps. "Your father called."

I sit up and throw off my covers. "Really? When?"

"A couple hours ago, after you cried yourself to sleep." She makes a sad face. "He said he was just calling to check on you."

I furrow my brows. "Why would he need to check on me? That's new."

"Maybe he's trying to be your father for once."

I get out of bed, seriously needing a shower. "Is Logan here?" I pull off my shirt then unbutton my jeans, kicking them off with my feet.

"No. He'll be here soon. Are you going to call your dad back?"

I don't even want to answer. I'm overwhelmed with everything else. "Man I stink. I'm going to go hop in the shower." My eyes water again, so I head to the bathroom, biting back a flood of tears.

The reality of what happened yesterday keeps flashing through my mind. I don't look at her, but softly say, "I'm not avoiding your question Gia, I just … I just need to deal with one thing at a time right now. Adding my father to the mix of everything that's going on is just too much for me to handle. You know what I mean?" She gets off my bed and pulls me into a big, warm hug. "I'll call him when I'm feeling better."

"I understand, completely." She pulls away, keeping her hands on my shoulders, and when I look into her eyes I can see the emotion in them. "You're a strong girl, Reese. You're going to get through this. Everything will work out." She means well, but I can't say that I agree.

After a long sulk in the shower, I put on a light blue tank and a pair of white boy shorts then tidy up my room to keep busy. Every other minute, I check my phone for a text or missed call, and every time, my heart breaks a little more when I don't see what I'm looking for.

"Reese," Gia calls from the other room. I throw the rest of my pillows on the bed then grab my phone and make my way over to join her. She's sitting on our couch in her pajamas, worrying her lip between her teeth, looking a little concerned. Then her eyes flick up, and she notices me standing beside her. "Logan just called," she pauses, and I can tell there's more she wants to say.

"And?" I arch a brow.

She scoots over and pats the spot next to her, and I take it. "Luke is with him. I guess he's not doing so well."

"Good. Neither am I. At least it shows he cares somewhat."

"He said he's wasted."

"What? Why is he driving?" I shake my head, surprised. "And why would Luke let him?"

"No Reese, not Logan. It's Luke. Luke is drunk."

Chapter Thirty-One

Reese

"Are you sure you heard him right?" I furrow my brows, confused. Luke doesn't drink. He told me he quit, long before he started the job at the gym. Then again, he said he wasn't fighting anymore either. Maybe he's just a pathological liar, and I fell victim to his lies.

"I guess they were involved in some kind of a bar fight," she murmurs.

"What?" My mouth drops. "Are they okay?"

"They're fine, but I'm not sure about the other man. Apparently Luke walked right up to him and knocked him out with just one punch. Logan said he wouldn't even give an explanation, just said the guy deserved it. Then he had to get him out of there before the police were called."

"Did the guy know who he was? Anybody could have recognized him." I run to my bedroom, digging through my closet for a sweatshirt and pants.

"No idea. What are you doing?" Gia asks, following behind me.

"I'm going to go wait outside." Sure, I'm angry with Luke, but it doesn't change the fact that I care about him—much more than I'd like to admit. His behavior has me worried. It's just not like him to do these kinds of things. At least I think it isn't.

"Wait. Let me get my shoes. I'll come with you," she replies. I watch her slide on a pair of pink flip-flops, and we make our way out the door. We cut through the grass and sit down next to the driveway in front of Luke's place. "Brr, it's cold out here," she says.

"Why didn't you grab a sweatshirt when we were inside?"

"Because I'm a dork and didn't think about it at the time," she grumbles. "I'll run back and get one real quick."

"Mine's big enough to share if you want," I reply. That's because it's Luke's, and I'm not going to give it back, even if he asks for it. It's the least he can do, since I gave him my heart—a shirt for a heart. I frown at the thought.

"Thanks, but I want my own." She shivers. "Be right back." She leaves me in total silence, except of course, for the crickets. I don't understand why she's so cold. It doesn't seem much cooler than last night. Then again, she was dressed in warmer pajamas and fuzzy green socks to keep her feet warm.

I drop my gaze to my bare toes then my heart rate picks up when I hear the sound of male voices in the distance, getting louder by the second. *Is that them? I thought they drove.* I glance over my shoulder, looking for Gia, but she's nowhere in sight. *How long does it take to find a flipping jacket?* Two male figures are headed my way, but it's hard to see them in the shadows.

On the outside, I try to stay calm. On the inside, I'm totally freaking out. Do I smile? Do I frown? Do I act like I don't care? What if I do care? *Where the hell is Gia?*

I step to the edge of the sidewalk as the figures come closer, trying to get a better look. "Well hello there," an unfamiliar voice says. I'm immediately aware that these men are not who I thought they were, and would bet, one of them is the new neighbor Gia was talking about.

"Sorry, I thought you were somebody else," I say politely, surprised by how much the man directly across from me resembles David Beckham. Gia was right, except I'm not noticing any tattoos.

He grins. "Must be a lucky guy." His eyes sparkle, and he has a nice smile, but it doesn't matter. I'm out here waiting for Luke. When I grin back and reach out my hand, Logan's truck comes around the corner, and I'm back to square one, hoping Gia will hurry her ass up.

"I'm Reese," I say quickly, attempting to look oblivious about the truck pulling up. "I live over there." I hear them closing their doors, and it only takes seconds before someone's walking toward us. The hair on the back of my neck stands up.

"Nice to meet you. I'm Sean, and this is Will." He nods his head toward his friend and still hasn't let go of my hand. "We live over there," he says, his grin growing wider. I know Luke's standing behind me. I can feel it, even before his hands grip my shoulders, and I turn around, looking into his eyes. They're glossy and focused on the two men standing across from me.

"Is there a problem, boys?" he asks in a menacing tone. I turn back around, mortified by the lethal stare he's pinning on them. They didn't do anything wrong. Then again, neither did I.

"We're all good over here," Sean replies evenly. "Just meeting our neighbor," He reaches out to shake Luke's hand. "Hi, I'm Sean. Don't you live over there?" he asks, pointing in the direction of Luke's condo.

Luke doesn't give him an answer. He doesn't even shake his hand. He just stands there and sizes him up. I'm completely shocked by his rudeness. "Will that be all?" he asks them.

"Luke," I say. "We were just introducing ourselves." He ignores me completely. His eyes never waver from their spot.

"Well it was nice to meet you Reese," Sean says. He glances up at Luke, and his eyes move to his friend, who stays completely quiet, as if he were watching a movie.

"Nice to meet you, too." I give a weak smile then mouth, "Sorry." He gives a slight nod.

"Maybe I'll see you around sometime," he says.

Luke chuckles behind me. "I don't think so, Sean. I'd stay away if you know what's good for you." *Oh God, could this be any more embarrassing?* Now I understand why he quit drinking.

We watch them walk away, then I quickly turn around and shoot him an evil glare. "To even think I was beginning to feel sorry for you, and then you go and behave like this!"

He still won't look at me. He's gazing over my head, clenching his fists at his sides and working his jaw when he says, "Wow, I didn't realize you'd move on so quick. It's fascinating."

I slap him. I slap him so hard, it hurts my hand, and I try to shake out the sting. "You have no right to say that to me! You did this!" I point at him, then turn around and walk as fast as I can to the house, but Luke is right behind me. He grabs me and spins me around before I can make it to the door.

"You want to hit me?" He puts his face right in front of mine. "Hit me. I deserve it," he begs, then takes my hand and brings it up to his face. His eyes are pleading. "Hit me again."

My eyes fill with tears, and the front door swings open. Logan walks out, pointing directly at me. "You two need to either settle this over here or over there," he says as he points at Luke's place. "Or soon we're going to have an audience." He opens the door wider. "Are you coming in?"

"Don't make me feel sorry for you. I don't want to feel sorry for you right now," I say quietly.

"Come over." He searches my face. "I don't know when I'll get to see you again. I need to be with you." He swallows loudly. "I know I don't deserve it, but I'm asking you, please just come over." The desperation in his voice and on his face makes it impossible for me to deny him.

"Okay, I'll come over."

"So you hit some innocent guy tonight?" I ask, getting comfortable on my favorite leather sectional. I meet his glossy red eyes, unable to look away as he leans against the door, watching me.

"I doubt he's innocent after what he did to you," he snorts.

I arch a brow, confused. "What he did to me? What you mean?"

"The guy with the big mouth," he grumbles. "The one who came into the restaurant. I don't regret it either." He rests the back of his head against the door and gazes at the ceiling.

I search my memory to find the person he's talking about. "You mean the guy with the messed up teeth? The one that was wearing the Packers hat?" I don't know why I'm surprised, and I'd be lying if I said it didn't make me feel all warm inside that he hit this man for me.

He crosses his arms, nodding once, and for a moment I wonder if he's standing there to keep his balance.

"I thought you quit drinking."

He shrugs. "I changed my mind." Damn, I'm feeling sorry for him again, even though he's the one who messed everything up. The thing is—I trust him with my life. I don't understand what's going on between us, but I know one thing's for sure: Luke would die for me.

I stand up and carefully walk over to him. His gaze feels like a caress. Although he smells like soap, the scent of liquor is apparent. I place my palm on the side of his face, noticing the light handprint from where I slapped him. "I did this." I look at him in question, but I already know the answer. I just feel bad that I gave it to him, though I had my reasons.

He clenches his jaw, leaning into my hand, then takes a step closer so that our toes are touching. "I didn't want to hurt you," he says softly before he reaches out and wraps his fingers in my hair. I love when he touches my hair; I love when he touches me period. I close my eyes, taking in the feel of his hands on me. I wasn't sure if I'd ever feel him again. "I hate what this is doing to you," he says and pulls me into a warm hug. "What it's doing to us."

He's holding me so tightly. I'm trying my best not to cry, but it feels like this is it—that this is our last night together. "Luke." I pull away and look at him. I think he's actually having a harder time holding it together than I am. Although it's somewhat comforting to see that he does really care, it doesn't help me fight my own tears that are now streaming down my face. "Why did you handle this the way you did? If you care about me as much as you say you do, then why?"

"I wish I could make you understand, but I can't. It's not something I can explain." He runs a hand through his hair, blowing out a breath. "I hope we can get past this, and one day you'll see that I had your best interest in mind."

My best, interest? I have no idea what this man is talking about. "What exactly do you mean by that?" I rub my temples out of irritation. "Waiting to tell me until two days before your departure? How is that in my best interest?"

He lifts my chin. "I told you. I can't explain everything right now, and none of it makes sense, but it will eventually."

I need to come out and say it—ask him the question I'm dreading most—but I'm terrified of his response. He's leaving tomorrow, and I'm not sure where we'll stand after this. I bring my shoulders back and say, "Is it because you're just not that *in* to me? Tell me the truth, Luke."

His eyes flare, and he backs me up so my body is pressed against the wall. "Not *in* to you?" he asks roughly as he frames me with his hands, leaning in closer. "I'm in love with you," he growls. "Can't you see that? I live and breathe you. I bleed you." His lips are so close to mine, and he stays there while I stand perfectly still, trying to catch my breath.

He's in love with me? My knees go weak, but he grips the back of my neck and brings his mouth to mine. A minute later, I reach over and pull off my sweatshirt, suddenly hot, still wearing my tank underneath it. His calloused hands frantically run over my skin in a way that he's never touched me. He nips at my bottom lip, then his tongue enters my mouth, and I welcome it with my own. My mind swirls with thoughts that this may be wrong. I pull away gasping, breathless. "Am I taking advantage of you? Because you've been drinking?" It was an honest question.

He chuckles into my mouth then swoops me up in his arms. I wrap my legs around him. "Man, you're cute," he says with a devilish grin. "The things you say sometimes. God, I'm going to miss you. All of you." At the same time I'm sinking into the mattress, my heart crumbles at the thought of him leaving tomorrow. I'm still upset and confused, but he's here and his hands are on me. I want to savor this moment, and he loves me. He *loves me.*

I lift up and kiss him with everything I have, then reach for his shirt, trying to pull it over his head. He helps me then throws it behind him. I run my fingers across the hard ridges of his stomach, and he closes his eyes, trembling at my touch. "Luke." He watches me from under his lashes, stroking my hair. I lift my arms up and gaze into his eyes, wanting him to see that I'm ready. There's confliction in his features, and I challenge him. "I'm ready," I say softly. He sucks in a breath before accepting my invitation.

As the cotton leaves my skin, a rash of tiny little bumps appear, taking its place. With heat in his gaze, he ever so slowly brushes the tips of his fingers down my neck. He moves over my shoulder, taking his time before he lightly grazes my collarbone. I'm entranced by the tenderness of it all, and shiver beneath his hands.

He watches my reaction so intently that I'm embarrassed. I know I can't hide the blush. "I'm going to miss this," he whispers, pressing his lips against my cheek then moving to my mouth, my neck, and every place his fingers traced before.

I whimper at the euphoria that's building in my body, and he pulls away with a feral growl, taking me in as if it's the last time he's going to see me. "You have no idea how much I want you," he says, there's warning in his voice. "But I can't take that from you tonight. Not yet." He leans over and pulls my bottom lip into his mouth, gently nipping at it with his teeth, then moves his body against me.

"Luke," I pant. The friction of his body pressed to mine feels incredible. "I'm not ready to stop." I don't want him to stop what he's doing—what we're doing.

He grips the back of my neck, gazing into my eyes. He's breathing just as hard as I am. "Don't take advantage of me." The corner of his mouth tips in a naughty grin. "I have a hard enough time resisting you when I'm sober." Then in a slow movement he places his hand against my neck and slides it down the center of my chest, before he peppers kisses along the line of my jaw, then up to my ear and whispers, "I want to make you feel good." His fingers graze over my skin, and he moves against me again, watching me closely as I whimper.

I may not have done this before, but I'm fully aware that what we're doing works both ways. "What about you?" I ask, but barely get the words out.

"Shh relax, Reese," he says, kissing me softly. "Let me take care of you." He rolls over and picks me up, placing me on his lap to where I'm straddling him. "Is this okay?" His voice alone is doing crazy things to me.

I gaze into the depths of his beautiful brown eyes. "It's perfect," I whisper. Then he leans forward and continues to kiss every inch of my neck, working his way to my shoulder as he pulls me against him. I moan at the sensation he's bringing me. It's almost too much. I'm terrified I might never get the chance to tell him how I feel. I don't know why, but it's a feeling that comes from deep down in my soul. I hold his face in my hands, and look into in those eyes again, as I move with him. "I love you. I love you, Luke Ryann."

He smiles then kisses the tip of my nose, moving over to my ear. "I need you to say it again."

"I love you." I'll say it a million times if he wants.

He grips my hips, pulling me in closer. I never want this to end. "Tell me you're mine," he says, running his hands over my shoulders, exploring more of my skin with his mouth. "No one else's. Tell me."

My entire body trembles, and my head falls back as I moan. "I'm yours. Only yours."

Last night couldn't have been any more perfect ... or so I thought. Now I'm sitting on the floor of Luke's closet, staring at the letter I've already dropped three times since I found it. My hands continue to shake from all the emotions flowing through me. I don't even know what to feel anymore. I've been lied to, by the person I trusted the most. I gave almost everything to him last night. When he said he loved me, I chose to believe him. He seemed so sincere, but it was a lie—all of it was a lie.

My eyes fall on the numbers typed in bold at the center of the paper—the date Luke is supposed to leave for Brazil, which happens to be more than three months away. So why did he leave today? And where did he go? And how did I overlook this the first time I read it? There's a loud knock on the door, but I don't get up to answer it. I just want to sit here, wrap my head around all of this, and stare at the damn letter.

"Reese," Gia calls, looking for me. I haven't seen her since last night when she left me. She was supposed to go grab a sweatshirt, but never came back outside.

"In here," I reply weakly, hoping that she can explain it in a way that would make him look innocent, but I know it's not going to happen.

She walks in and tilts her head to the side. "What are you doing in the closet?"

I hand over the letter and stare at the floor. "The date," I murmur. "He's been lying." My eyes fill with tears. "I don't think he went to Brazil."

Chapter Thirty-Two
Luke

"And you're sure she has no idea?" Andrew asks me. It bothers me since I've already answered this question. There's no way I'd let her in on what we're doing. I don't want her involved—in any way, shape, or form.

I look him straight in the eye. "For the second time, she doesn't know. It's too dangerous."

"Did you use the excuse we discussed?"

"Actually no. Something else came up, and I just went with it."

"What'd you tell her?"

I'm reminded of the pain I saw in her features and the tears I watched her cry. I hate it. I hate that this is hurting her—that I'm hurting her. "Told her I took a job in Brazil."

He nods; rubbing the stubble on his chin, he reaches over and pats me on the back, saying, "We'll get him." He presses his lips into a tight line. "Just don't do anything stupid. I need to bring you back in one piece if I ever want to know my daughter again."

If you enjoyed Raising Ryann, please don't forget
to leave a review!

Be on the lookout for Book #2
in the Bad Boy Reformed series,
Resisting Ryann, coming spring 2014.

Acknowledgements

First and foremost I have to mention my best friend Camryn Pinner, for the countless number of days and nights you helped me work on this story. You were the first person to put your faith in me, and stuck by me through this entire process. I can never thank you enough. To my husband for playing Mr. Mom- taking care of our children and cleaning up after their messes, while I spent several hours a day, holed up in the den. Thank you for allowing me this time to fulfill my dream. To my children for their patience with my truckload of excuses, as to why, I need more time on the computer. To all my loyal fans from Wattpad, you know who you are. Thank you for supporting me, even though I didn't post the entire book, which made some people very angry. Your encouraging comments are what pushed me to continue forward, and believe in myself. To the rest of my fans, thank you so much for taking a chance with me, and picking up my story. To my copyeditor Madison Seidler, thank you for finding, and fixing all, of my mistakes, and for making me seem smarter than I really am. I appreciate your hard work. To Sarah Hansen for my beautiful cover art. I'm so glad I found you and look forward to using you again. Also, I'd like to send a big thanks to Angela McLaurin for using your talent by making my book look pretty on the inside. To my parents and sisters for putting up with me, when I'm being a pain in the rear. And last but not least, to my Lord and Savior Jesus Christ, for loving me unconditionally, even with all my imperfections, which are many.

About the Author

Wife. Mother. Writer. Reader. Dreamer.

For more information on Alyssa Rae Taylor you can visit her here:

https://www.goodreads.com/alyssaraetaylor

https://www.facebook.com/authoralyssaraetaylor

https://twitter.com/Alyssartaylor

https://www.alyssaraetaylor.com

CPSIA information can be obtained
at www.ICGtesting.com
Printed in the USA
LVOW11s0902120117
520665LV00002BA/162/P